CW00504049

From the Author of *Take Three Boys*

THE WAY IT IS

Rita Trotman

Copyright belongs to Rita Trotman 2018

The right of Rita Trotman to be identified as the Author of the Work has been asserted by her in accordance with the Copyright, Designs and Patents Act 1988

Apart from any use permitted under UK copyright law, this publication may only be reproduced, stored or transmitted in any form with prior written permission from the author.

All characters in this publication are fictitious.

Also by this author 'Take Three Boys' available as an ebook

All proceeds to The Joseph Foundation

For Eric

The Way It Is

When Alfie and Saskia cross social boundaries, the combination of teenage love, drink and drugs turns life into chaos. Shocked by their actions, both mothers struggle to deal with the fallout.

Laden with guilt, Lottie and Tracey set out to rescue their kids from life- threatening situations. Each has her own perspective on the disastrous liaison and there are no connective strands.

When one catastrophe is dealt with, another takes its place. Can both mothers change their pre-conceived ideas about the other and learn to live in harmony? Someone special hopes they can.

Mummy... it was cold...really cold...it felt... like... I was in a fridge... And there was... something wet and sticky on my pink dress... the new one....you know?... the one you bought me for Gemma's party. I... I wore it to look grown-up for Alfie. I'm sorry... I know you're mad at me...My head was all over the place...I remember screaming at Alfie to leave me alone...I was feeling odd and...I didn't know what I was saying. I could see blue lights and there was shouting but.... I couldn't think straight...everything was... like... in bright colours and there were shapes and patterns on the walls. I want to come home to you and Daddy but...I can't find a way.

Lottie

It was roll-of-the-dice morning. Roll a six and I'd get up, anything else was licence to stay in bed. Well, it went something like that in the fuzziness I called my brain. While our daughter was kept from us, the duvet had the appeal of a double gin and tonic most mornings. But I dragged one weary leg after the other and made a deal with myself, (or was it with God?) - get dressed by nine and spend time in Saskia's room. I'd ring fenced the pleasure to encourage a more normal routine. Small steps, but it was reward enough to inhale the scent of my daughter, to lie on her bed and hug her pillow. Until she came home, Saskia's bedroom was all I had to cling to.

Her white polar bear lay exactly where she'd left him. Wisps of stuffing bulged from his belly where she'd over-indulged a bear that was more cuddly-dog than carnivore. I cradled him in my arms but he offered no relief. Then, as I lay on her bed and snuggled into her duvet, I heard her voice. I knew my delusion made me a fruit cake, but I didn't care. Her crystal tones were fuelled with irritation. *'Knock Mummy. Please knock when you come into my room.'* And although hearing her voice was whimsical fancy, I settled for whatever helped me through those dark days.

1

I opened her wardrobe and analysed her colour-coordinated clothes. Piles of pink tee shirts blended with dresses and shoes, each pair in its original box. The perfume we gave her for Christmas was the over-riding scent of my daughter; I snagged a pink jumper and buried my nose in it but quickly dampened the expensive mohair.

That day showered on auto-pilot before slumping downstairs to make a cup of black coffee. I day-dreamed a bit and imagined a phone call to say Saskia was back with us. When I checked the answerphone, there was no news but I was good at dealing with disappointment. It wasn't until I grabbed my handbag and car keys that I realised I'd made a decision; maybe it was life-changing, it was certainly the first decision of any merit for weeks.

The morning traffic was unusually sluggish and my blood pressure drifted; I had a pulse that threatened a headache. Of course, I could have wimped-out and turned off the by-pass for home, but my sensible-self knew I should keep the appointment. It would please Tom, if nothing else.

Tom, both husband and best friend, was the stalwart who'd dragged me through the dark weeks. He was so much stronger than me and coped better on a daily basis. But occasionally I caught him off-guard; I saw hurt etched in his face and sadness soaked his eyes with unshed tears. Much as I wanted to, I had nothing in my emotional box-of-tricks to offer him.

My arrival in the carpark was more serendipity than a deliberate act. I parked, turned off my phone and took a deep breath. I'd promised Tom I'd bring an open mind to this appointment, so I ventured forth with my handbag and a good attitude.

Inside the neo-classical building I gazed around the waiting-room. The blonde wood furniture and designer cushions were too twee for my taste and the lull of background music was beginning to jar. I wanted to smother the pretty receptionist with her perfect hair and makeup, although I knew that was off -the-scale of reasonable. She didn't even have a bloody wrinkle.

I was asked to take a seat. The grey washed walls and framed landscapes should have soothed, but instead they reminded me of the art in Harrods's which Saskia loved to browse. She was convinced she could spot the next Banksy. But even that fleeting memory of my daughter threated to rock my self-control, so I studied the water cooler and counted the stack of plastic cups until I got bored at number twenty three. The room had all the ambiance of a dentist's waiting room for fruit-loops. When I passed through the oak door to consult 'Dr Nancy Edmunds,' I could no longer deny my life was in crisis. I would be committing myself to a process as alien as landing on Mars.

I picked up a copy of Vogue and allowed brief respite from the pain that defined me. My eyes swam across the crowing headline about someone's fantastic life, but I had no appetite for the rich and famous. I discarded the magazine and browsed my own life instead – my happy life with Tom and Saskia. But just as I'd focused on a chubby, four year old dancing in a field of poppies somewhere in France, the aroma of Columbian coffee hauled me back to reality. Ten minutes had slipped by and the wrinkle-free eye candy brought me sustenance with a smile that lit her face. I glanced at the indulgent biscuits with distaste. My stomach threatened to return anything I placed near my mouth; I had as much control over my body as bloody Alice when she tumbled down a rabbit- hole. Even worse, I had no idea if the Mad Hatter or the Cheshire cat lurked behind the oak door.

I eyed the closed door and realised for the first time, I was someone who needed mending. A rush of humiliation crept up my neck. I wondered if the clever, highly-recommended doctor would emerge and decide I should be sectioned.

Too soon the door stood ajar and sunlight washed the carpet to a rice- pudding smudge. The air was rinsed with camomile or maybe rose? Who cared? I stepped inside a room with a décor intended to soothe ruffled souls, but it didn't soothe me.

I managed a weak smile as the doctor enticed me in with the enthusiasm of a party host. From her low-heeled pumps to the silk scarf draped around her over-fifties neck-wrinkles, there was nothing to intimidate. Nancy wasn't paid to intimidate.

I looked around but found no point of reference. It was a mystery why I'd laid myself open to a stranger who would delve into my life with the stringency of squeezed lemons. And could I expect her to re-balance the strips of matter that used to be me? Probably not.

The life-fixer sashayed across the room and adjusted window blinds to exclude bothering shards of light. A smile broke through pink lips but didn't reach her eyes.

'So... Lottie. Are you quite comfortable? There's water on the side.'

I was mesmerised by a pair of blown-glass doves on a side table. Llalique I guessed. Then I pulled myself back to reality.

'Thank you. That's kind.'

I gulped at the water as if it was a stiff gin and tried to swallow my fear. I felt guilty for not giving her my full attention, but reasoned for a hundred and ten pounds an hour, I could do what I bloody well liked.

I thought of Tom who was always there for me. To my amazement, soon after we lost Saskia he'd thrown himself into the rigours of boarding school life. It was unimaginable to me how he could teach history to upper-crust kids when his own child was struggling for life. But when I saw the harnessed tears, I knew he was hurting too.

A robin on the bird table distracted me. It was a youngster, I noted, a feisty fledgling brave enough to see off the sparrows.

Over the years, Tom and I had grown together like Lego. 'A tight fit' my mum called us. But he was at a loss to deal with... my depression....anguish or any other label anyone wished to bestow on me. He was caring and in his gauche way, would have dunked me in lemonade if he thought it would help.

For days Tom tried to instil in me the importance of engaging with the counselling process. I think he'd taken advice from a colleague as we didn't mix in circles where counselling was an everyday occurrence. Tom suggested I needed an outlet to talk about my feelings. Not a turn of phrase usually forthcoming from my husband. 'She'll need to know the details, Snooks. Tell her how life has been for you. She'll want to help.' Maybe her fees had something to do with that.

Nancy was waiting and I sensed it was my turn to speak. But what the hell was I supposed to say?

'Have you ever been in therapy before?'

I shook my head with the vigour of someone asked if they smoked pot. Still as a cobra she studied me. I knew she was judging; she'd probably noted my lack of makeup, scruffy blue jeans and a linen shirt on its second outing that week. Perhaps my designer handbag, lying in a pliable drape at my feet would redeem me; it was a remnant of a past life when such things mattered. She started writing. Probably logging that her client was stressed, but it didn't take rocket science to spot that. She browsed my notes, checking my age, I guessed. I was a good decade younger than her although no one would have known by the road atlas I saw on my face, when I dared to look in a mirror.

I knew I was scowling, I'd been scowling for weeks, but I didn't care. I knew I was displaying closed body-language, but I didn't care about that either. She'd have seen it a hundred times before. There was a silence but it wasn't comfortable and I was aware her fees were accruing minute by expensive minute. As someone brought up to appreciate money, I found it hard to squander it and this session already felt an indulgence. I noticed my file of notes was thin. Not much to show for a family tragedy. Nancy looked up and gave me a smile, presumably to encourage dialogue.

I had no idea what to say. I was a counselling virgin and almost ready to sign out on this project.

After several minutes Nancy gave up on my ability to communicate and tried a gentle nudge.

'How long have you and your family lived at Churchill's College, Lottie?'

I pondered the answer. 'About fourteen years. Saskia was two.'

'Quite an unusual life, I should think, caring for all those wealthy, boys.'

'We like it.'

Nancy clearly hoped for better. What did she want? Did she need me to tell her we had a privileged lifestyle? Everyone for miles around knew that. I wasn't making it easy but only because I had no idea how the session should evolve.

'Would you like to talk about today? How things are today, Lottie? There was no hint of impatience in her voice.

I met her eyes while my brain worked overtime. I was thinking, *life's crap, isn't it? Just like yesterday,* but I redacted it, 'Pretty much like every day since it happened. Rubbish.'

'Mm'.

Clearly 'rubbish' was not a technical term she recognised. She pinned me with her professional eye contact.

'Have you tried the relaxation methods I recommended in my Notes of Introduction? They can be helpful before your first appointment.'

I gulped at the glass of water like a stranded goldfish as my eyes met hers over the glass. 'Not really.' *Bloody relaxation exercises? Is she kidding?* I obviously wasn't therapy material. Tom worried it could be too much mumbo-jumbo and maybe he was right. But I took a deep breath and gave it another go. 'Some days I can barely get out of bed,' I offered. 'Hardly conducive to *'doing exercises'*, do you think?' I sounded spiky but it was the best I had to offer. And then out of nowhere I felt a wobble coming on. There was something about that place that stripped dignity. It was worse than a dentist's waiting room.

'No. No it's not.' She smiled again, clearly spotting my distress.

I wondered idly if the bill was calculated on a points system; maybe it was based on the number of smiles she bequeathed on her clients. When did I become such a cynic?

'Maybe you're not quite ready.' Nancy manoeuvred a seamless change of direction. 'Shall we talk about being kind to you? And the need to grieve? Both are crucial in the early days.'

My gaze wandered around the room. I was expecting something better. Instant gratification would have been nice.

'You need to guard against submerging your feelings, Lottie. You must allow grief to take its course,' Nancy continued. 'Are you able to talk about Saskia...to Tom? To friends...perhaps? Talking about Saskia is therapeutic. It helps the grieving process.'

'Grieve? How can I grieve for her?' My voice reached several decibels above my usually moderated tone. I gulped a raw sob down my throat which met a knot of anger rising from my stomach. Something threatened to escape like a jack-in-the-box and needed containing for, once released, it would never climb back in.

Nancy waited. She was paid to wait, wasn't she? Tick, tick. Another thirty pounds.

'Saskia's not dead you know.' I adopted a tone more suited to addressing a child. It was my default mode as I was well versed in dealing with children. 'She's not...anything, is she'? I dabbed belligerently at my face and knew I'd made it red and blotchy. I tried again. 'My beautiful sixteen year old daughter is...just not home with us...She's not where she belongs.'

Nancy offered her sympathetic face. I thought she'd make a good funeral director. And then suddenly, irrationally, I found Alfie Collings playing hard-ball with what was left of my brain. I'd banned that yob from my head-space weeks before to save my sanity. Bloody Alfie Collings! I even hated the sound of his name. He was a lad who'd been dragged up by some dead-end family and had the audacity to lure my daughter into his grubby little world. Now, she might never be my Saskia again.

When I was a child my Dad used to mutter, 'I'll swing for him.' He'd shake his hazel stick at a lad helping in the school holidays and get red in the face. But no matter how hard I tried, my childish mind couldn't picture Dad in the playpark. Now I understood exactly what he'd meant all those years ago, and I knew I'd damage Alfie Collings if I ever got my hands on him.

I was thirsty Mummy. My throat was so dry I could have emptied an ice bucket down it but... I couldn't see water anywhere. I think I was in a sort of gym-store. There were balls and mats around...

And I didn't feel like moving or trying to come home. I was so cold and there must have been blood on my fingers 'cos the smell was the same as when I get a nosebleed. I knew you'd be furious with me for staying out so late...it was just...my body felt fuzzy and limp... I needed help but...I couldn't do anything about it. I cried for you and Daddy but then I remembered you wouldn't come 'cos you had no idea where I'd gone. I know this is my fault. I'm so sorry Mummy.

I was livid with myself for crying in front of a psychologist. Normally, I wouldn't allow such loss of control. I rummaged in my bag for tissues and found them right at the bottom next to lip balm and my car keys which were attached to a fat, black and white cow with an enormous udder. Mum and Dad had put the key ring in my stocking one Christmas and explained it was for *the girl who had everything.* I visualised my lovely Dad with his weathered, smiling face and realised he'd hate to see me so distressed. He was the man who sacrificed everything for me to have a successful life; he was the father who pushed and encouraged me to be the best I could be, and when I became the polished specimen, he did nothing but worry about me. Parents eh?

Dad thought I'd never get used to living *'with the gentry in that posh school of yours,'* but I did. It took a while to meld into the upper-class ways of Churchill's College, although I was supported all the way by Tom, who'd been born to it. He knew all the weird and wonderful routines of Churchill's and took pleasure in my slow initiation. But happy as the early years of our marriage were, they were not fulfilled as our desire to be parents always sat like a threatening cloud above our lives. I never knew when it might rain. The worst times were the early losses of little blobs, too small to be called babies. But they were always a baby to me. And then, one day, after years of heartache, everything was perfect. We adopted Saskia and our lives were complete.

Damn! I realised Nancy had spoken and I'd missed it. Again. 'For God's sake,' I heard myself say. I was past caring. 'Grieving is for the dead. Well it is in our family.' I swallowed hard, searching for a grasp on my dignity. 'She's not dead. My Saskia's not dead.' Unfettered tears ran down my face.

'Grieving comes in many forms, Lottie,' the paid-to-be-patient Nancy offered.

I noticed the strands of grey at her temples and wondered when she'd get her roots done. Her voice took on a softer timbre.

'You've suffered loss, even though Saskia is still with us. Loss of Saskia as you knew her.' She sat in silence while I digested the wisdom.

I needed to make a contribution so I swallowed hard and took a breath. 'I've hardly cried. Not properly...until now. I've been too bloody angry to cry.' I knew I sounded pathetic but it was the best I could do.

Nancy remained silent, she watched as tears from a deep, dark place, washed down my cheeks. I was thinking this an expensive session if I could only cry and shout. I never shouted. But maybe this woman had no idea what being in a coma was like. *Well tell her then Snooks.* I could sense Tom urging me on.

'She's poked full of plastic tubes,' I began. 'She's fed through a tube, she pees through a tube and she's breathing courtesy of a machine.' Nothing was forthcoming from Nancy and I wasn't sure if I could carry on. The pain was palpable and I was breathing in short, shallow gasps. Was I having a panic attack? I managed to knit a few more words together. 'Saskia is alive, but... only because other people choose it.' I dabbed at tears which had a life of their own. 'What if they decide to switch her off?' I'd strung together eight little words and crumpled with the agony of them; I bled from their very formation.

Nancy nodded her understanding and indicated a box of tissue beside me. I heard a whine and found it was coming from my own mouth. 'Tom's getting on with his life and I can't bear that,' I bleated like a three-year-old who'd had their sweets stolen. I thought of Tom who was teaching a group of over-privileged boys at that precise moment, none of whom had slipped into a coma in the last few weeks. I realised self-pity would have been an easy route to take. 'It makes me so angry,' I told Nancy. 'Unreasonably angry.' I gulped and tried to grab a semblance of self-respect.

'It's Tom's way of coping Lottie. He probably needs to be busy. That's how some men cope with trauma. Do you and Tom talk about Saskia? About your hopes for her future?' It's really important that you keep talking to each other.'

'We do, when he's at home but...everything seems so ...I don't know...tense...everything makes me angry.' I caught the content of my nose with a tissue taken from the box on the glass coffee table. In that environment 'man sized' would have done a better job. I failed to harness an unattractive sniff or reign in the raging emotions and still little of value was forthcoming from the counsellor. And the bill was escalating minute by expensive minute.

'She lied to us.....she slipped out to meet this...this yob who enticed her to a party. It was a drug-fuelled party and that's why I'm so bloody angry.'

Nancy watched me struggle.

'And there's the guilt. I didn't know what she was up to.' I wiped more mucous from my face. 'I'm her mother. I'm supposed to know. I'm supposed to keep her safe.'

Nancy waited. I had no idea what for. Until I completely broke down? There was another silence.

'Mothering isn't a perfect science Lottie. And piling guilt onto unhappiness is never fruitful. Anyone can be deceived by teenagers. They specialise in covering their tracks.'

I was beginning to wonder if that was it. Was that the sum total I could expect from the clever Nancy? *Anyone can be deceived by teenagers?*

'Shit. Do you know what? I don't need this.' I had no idea where it sprang from. 'I can talk to myself at home, thank you. I can come up with statements like that. And for free.' I grabbed my handbag and left the room as mumbled apologies dripped into soggy tissues.

'Send my husband the bill,' I threw at the Receptionist as I exited into the brightness of a sunny day.

Tracey

Whichever way I argued it, bumble-bee wasn't a good look. Spindly legs in yellow and black striped tights never looked right on a grown-up. No wonder they were cheap. But while I was sprawled on a dusty floor, they made me look like a performing puppet with me strings missing. I should have thought more about what I put on that morning, I knew Dickie couldn't stand stripes. Nor the clinging yellow jumper, bobbled from too much washing. And my black skirt had risen like a flood tide on the Thames, it was right up 'round me ass. My Alfie would have floored Dickie if he knew he'd hit me.

The row started while I was cleaning Dickie's flat. He'd yelled at me to get him a couple of cans of beer from the corner shop and I got lippy 'cos it was eleven o'clock already and I hadn't even started the hoovering. Anyway, when I was cleaning for him out of the goodness of me heart, I wanted him out from under me feet, not slurping beer around the place. Stupid as I was, I argued and told him to get his own beer.

I noticed the twitch of his mouth which usually meant he was angry. He always got a bit red in the face when he was about to blow; his eyes went hard and he sweated over his top lip. It was a funny sort of look he got when his temper was up. I should have clocked it.

He came at me like a raging bull. God knows where an old man stores all that anger, probably the same place he keeps his brains. Wherever it came from, it was quick to spew over and I took the full force.

I tried to keep me balance when I saw him coming but he knocked me to the floor, he flicked me to one side like a bleeding Christmas-tree fairy. I bounced off the wall and went down like a sack of spuds and forgot to tidy away me skinny legs in the heat of the moment. Even though I knew they aggravated the hell out of him. 'God certainly had a sense of humour when he made you,' he said. 'Let's have a freak in Alton Street.' Oh yes, and then he said, 'let's make a tart to keep the world amused. Let's give 'er long skinny arms and legs with a life of their own'. Dickie was a real shit sometimes.

I must have hit the back of my hand on the radiator when I went down, but it didn't feel serious even though it was bleeding. Dickie looked at his handiwork; he was about six foot above me towering like King Kong. I could only see his ear and some scraggy hair but I knew he'd be taking in every miserable detail. A bruise was swelling over me left eye and it felt like it would close. Didn't feel it happen, but I guessed it was his fist what did it. My ankle was twisted awkward too and my heart was thumping like I'd run the hundred metres.

I glanced at my wristwatch. Just to pass the time really - wasn't going nowhere and not expecting a number nine bus through any time soon. My Lily's Mickey Mouse watch made me smile, despite myself. She lent it me when mine gave up the ghost a week or so before 'cos she knew I couldn't afford a new one, even when the housing benefit came in. 'You'll need it Mum, 'cos you can't be late for work.' She's very clever, my little Lily. I took it from her and gave her a hug. Told her she could stay up late and watch TV on the weekend. Meanwhile I was wallowing like a helpless minnow on the floor when I should've been trying to get my Alfie out of prison.

Dickie's angry face was glowering at me as I sniffed and snivelled at his feet. But I was afraid to get up. I must have banged me head 'cos I felt sick, but I tried to ignore it. The whole thing was embarrassing enough for a grown-up mother of two kids, without me throwing vomit over his feet.

I squeezed my eyes tight shut 'cos I wouldn't let him see me cry. I didn't reckon tears and my snotty nose would look good together. And Dickie still hadn't moved. Looking at me mousy, short hair which hadn't been washed for days and me ugly face without a smear of makeup. My bitten finger nails were curled into me palms and I 'spose I gave him all the reasons he needed to treat me like shit.

'Just look at you Trace. Look at you. You're a bloody mess'.

He nudged my ribs with his boots which made me gasp. Unfortunately, I caught sight of me reflection in the wardrobe mirror and couldn't argue with him. A pink flush had crept up my neck and something screamed 'loser' in a voice that was louder than Ken Bruce who was rattling-on in the kitchen.

Maybe wearing something more grown up might have helped. Perhaps the blue denim dress I elbowed away from a yummy-mummy in the charity shop a few days before would have been better than bumblebee. But I knew I was kidding myself; I'd have been lying at his feet, whatever I wore.

My hand was still bleeding. I eyeballed the blobs of red stuff that oozed from a sizeable cut and dared them to multiply. I'd got enough to cope with, without me hand giving in to a pathetic bleed.

He hadn't moved. Still the pasty-face was staring down at me under a cloud of muddy frizz. He usually had a lot more to say, but the lack of a few pints inside him kept him almost civil. His feet were a worry though. A kick in the head wasn't out of the question if I dared move or give him any more lip.

'How do you reckon you're going to help your Alfie? You can barely look after yerself.'

That made me all the more determined. I'd show him what a mother can do when her kid's in trouble. It was more than just trouble though wasn't it? My Alfie was in prison.

I'd never lived up to Dickie's expectations, to say nothing of me own, but I was determined to show him I could do better. OK, so I wasn't that bright and I did have a meltdown now and then. Mum said I changed when the moon was full but I knew that was a load of crap. She had some funny ideas, had me mother. But I was going to help my boy, you could bet on that.

I wanted to get up. My face itched and I was cold, but I didn't want to risk his number elevens again. The slime was tight on me skin, a bit like the day they made me run the half-marathon at school, even though I had a letter from Mum to say I had me period. My face was blotched and ugly that day too, I was smeared with sweat, tears of humiliation and the remains of bottled water someone chucked over me. It was meant to cool me down, they said. But it turned out it wasn't sweat when Dickie hit me - well maybe some, and probably lots of snot too, but something else was drying in the mix and I wondered if I'd need a stitch or two.

'Why do you make me do these things Trace? You make me so bloody angry.'

Everything made Dickie angry.

'Don't just lie there. Get up you stupid bitch or I'll give you something to really grizzle about'.

I wasn't getting up, well not straight away, and 'e didn't give me something else to grizzle about. He went to the pub.

'Don't know when you're well off, that's your trouble,' he chucked over his shoulder, like I was listening.

The door slammed and he was gone. I crawled to the chest of drawers and pulled myself up. Everything hurt, including me pride, so I went home. I thought, bugger his cleaning, he can do it himself.

Old Man Nesbit was coming down the street on his way to get his pension but I didn't look at him. I shuffled past him and he didn't so much as look my way. I let myself into me flat and put the kettle on for a cuppa and after a quick grope in the bathroom cabinet for Aspirin. Then I took me cup of tea and crawled into Alfie's bed. It felt safe in Alfie's bed though who knew when he was likely to want it again. Stuck in that prison, he hadn't been home for weeks. It wasn't right, him being in there 'cos both me and Lily missed him. Even a tear-away like my Alfie could be missed.

Alfie had a life that was all his own. From a young age he went to unknown places with people I knew nothing about. The street kids were cock-of-the-walk around our way and Alfie was top-dog for years. I lost control of him when he didn't need money from me no more. I knew I should have asked questions about all his dosh; there was a lot of it and it couldn't have been legal. But somehow I never managed to find the right time. So Alfie ran wild from the age of ten. I wasn't much more than a kid meself.

I slipped between the sheets, gentle so as not to hurt me head. Alfie's bed was a tad crusty. 'Ripe' Mum would have called it, and his room was a mess, mostly 'cos he hadn't let me in to clean it properly for years. He was afraid I'd find

15

his dope. Like I didn't know about his dope. You could smell it out in the hall.

The thing was, I needed to get Alfie out of that prison and it was all I could think about. I was convinced he never hurt that girl but he had no one to speak up for him. Where were all his big-shot friends when he needed them? There had to be something I could do, but I was damned if I knew what.

He was a great little kid, before he went wild. I used to love our teatimes together - that can be special for a single Mum. I'd pump him for information about his day. 'What was for dinner then?' He'd huff a bit. 'Dunno. Can't remember.'

Mum never asked *me* them sorts of questions. She was too busy with her latest bloke, probably. 'Did you play football today then?' 'Aw Mum! It's Thursday. We never play on Thursday'. His little face would screw up 'cos I'd forgotten his football day.

I'd have loved to watch Alfie play games at school like some of the other mums. I'd have hollered at the top of my lungs, 'Go Alfie go!' Trouble was, I never fitted in with the other mothers. 'Coon lover' they called me and who was I to deny it with my Alfie like a little milk chocolate drop? I tried once or twice to get into conversation with them but I skulked away when they kept collaring me about Alfie's antics. 'See this bruise? I'll bruise *his* bleeding face if he touches my Ruby again.' And the snotty cow from the hardware shop said, 'I'll have you know my Dan ain't got nits, nor never had. Lying little sod your Alfie is. Cried all night my Dan did.'

I used to take Alfie to the park on Saturdays and his little legs raced over the grass like his life depended on it. We used to feed the ducks on weekends. His black curls tumbled over his eyes and his chubby little legs bobbed along like a Labrador puppy. I used to dream he could be the next Maradonna.

The Way It Is

I could feel blood had dripped from my eyebrow and reached somewhere near my top lip. I couldn't lick it. I hated the metallic taste of blood, 'specially when it was mine. I sniffed Alfie's cold, smelly sheets with more relish than was healthy for a mother, but I could smell my Alfie and any grain of comfort was welcome. I knew I should have stripped his bed weeks before but I hadn't been able to do it. And I was glad I hadn't washed my Alfie away. The thought of his clinging scent being washed down the drain was too much to bear. There was more than a grain of comfort to be had in the smell of Alfie.

I kept churning things over but I was none the wiser about what would happen to him in prison. They took him into custody after problems at his party. Little fool! What was he thinking? Why would he take a girl from that snooty college to his party? As if there weren't enough girls round our way to choose from. I knew no good would come of it when he started doing his painting at that la-de-da college. 'Painting pictures is for play-school,' I told him, but he never listened to me, and see where that got him. They said Alfie stabbed her but I didn't believe the fuzz. My Alfie was no saint - far from it, but he wasn't a killer, neither.

I tried to sleep but couldn't settle. And even though I was resting, I had to keep a close eye on the time 'cos I wanted to be at school when Lily came out. The kids were all I seemed to worry about.

My hand stopped bleeding and I changed the plaster but I had one hell of a headache. I took more painkillers and decided I'd change Alfie's sheets after all. I knew I'd regret it but they were stinking and it wasn't like he was coming home any time soon.

I was still a bit shook-up and I must have looked like hell on legs. Me headache shifted a bit and I didn't feel sick any more. I'd slapped a plaster on me face too and knew I should probably have got checked out, but I couldn't be doing with those nurses at A&E who always looked at you like yer were road-kill.

It was pissing with rain - I could hear it on the concrete path outside Alfie's window and I wondered if Dickie would come to babysit as usual so I could go to work. I hated being nice to him, 'specially after what he'd done to me, but I was all out of choices. After I'd given Lily her tea I had the office cleaning to do. I needed the money and at least I'd get home in time to see her to bed.

Me cleaning job was important and helped me manage a bit better. I was saving for Lily's school trip and she needed new clothes; her feet grew like an elephant. I had to manage me money better 'cos the Social had got me on their books and I was never going to let them have a pop at me, not if I could help it.

I knew my face was a mess 'cos I could feel the swelling and one eye had closed. And there was a fuckin' great lump on me forehead. Not that anybody would notice 'cos I'd pull me hoodie up and wait on the other side of the road for Lily, away from the other parents. Later, I'd slip through the streets to me job with me anorak hood up so no one would take any notice of me. The office girls would be long gone. All tits and teeth they were. Giggled like schoolgirls in their smart clothes, whiffing of cheap perfume and makeup. They never gave me a look but I was worried the factory caretaker might clock me black eye and bloody wounds. He'd want to fuss and send me to hospital to be checked over and start talking about ringing the nearest women's refuge. I couldn't be doing with all that.

I needed to shower and get some clothes from me room. I wondered if I should let Lily have Alfie's room now he didn't need it. She only had a box room which was more suited to a gerbil. But that was like saying I'd given up on Alfie, it was as if he'd never come home. I couldn't do that. Lily could manage where she was for a while longer.

It was a troubled path my Alfie took while he was growing up. Suppose having a thirteen year old mother never helped the poor little bugger. Actually I was fourteen when he was born and Mum agreed to keep him 'til I was sixteen. Then she told me I was on me own. I thought about adoption but I'd never been able to live with meself if I'd given him away. Mum wanted an abortion soon as she knew, but I told her to take a running jump. Alfie's father was no help either. Tall dark and lush 'e was. I couldn't take me eyes off him in the beginning and he liked young, blonde girls. Back then I suppose I was jail bait. I was too young to be doing it and not old enough to know better. As it turned out, he ended up in prison for burglary and never come out. Well he did come out, but it was in a box. Another inmate was done for his murder and I didn't want my Alfie to know about that.

I knew Alfie's problems were my fault but I'd never known how to be a good mother. And now he was banged up and his brief said there wasn't much chance of bail. My boy didn't even want me to visit him which broke me heart. Mum said he was probably embarrassed for me to see him in that place. I dunno about that, but I was determined to see him anyway.

Until he was about eight, Alfie always wanted to be with me. Real close we were. But when he got to about nine or ten, things changed. Couldn't put me finger on it but he sort of grew up overnight. I reckoned it was the crowd he hung about with, older lads who were up to no good. Alfie would come home late and never told me what he'd been up to. More than once the police brought him home but he wasn't scared of no one.

Alfie had a bit of respect for Old Dickie at first, but even that disappeared as he got older. I 'spose, looking back, he worked out a way to do pretty much what he wanted; I was such a lousy mother. I was usually at work and when I wasn't, some bloke was taking my attention and I'd be turning a trick to put food on the table. I was no different from me bleeding mother.

My Alfie learnt from a young age the ins and outs of what people did in bed. At first, he asked about the grunting and giggling he heard over the cartoons on TV when I had punters in. Later, curiosity kicked-in and he constructed a system of planks and bricks outside my bedroom window to get a look at the goings-on; that was the trouble with a ground-floor flat, there was no privacy. I suppose he was looking for stuff to amuse his mates. He wanted to grow up too quick in my book, but I soon got his measure. Being kids, they couldn't keep quiet and I clocked them good and proper. The bloke I was with gave me a slap for me trouble and never paid me. I gave Alfie the beating of his life; I guess I should have done it sooner but it didn't seem to make any difference. He wasn't like his sister. My Lily could quote all the rights and wrongs of the Children's Act, so I'd never have dared touch her. Not that she needed it. But Alfie took the punishment and then, I 'spose, he put his mind to working out another scam to make a few quid for a bottle of cider and a few fags.

When Old Dickie first tipped up at our house Alfie thought he was a sad old bastard who'd crept round me and wheedled his feet under me table. Dickie had a flat in Skankland, (postal address is Newman Court,) which is just round the corner from me and I'd seen him around for most of me life. Mum knew him and never said anything bad about him so that was something. Alfie was a bit wary at first, but I realised Dickie could be a big help when he offered to babysit, 'specially as I'd just got a job at the corner shop. Lily was too little to leave at home and Mum, true to her word, had washed her hands of us. And for a while I managed to come off the game. I knew it was bad for the kids to see the goings on, but I needed money and I was desperate to keep the kids with me; the social were razor-sharp at removing kids, back then.

One day Alfie asked me if Dickie was my boyfriend. At first I thought he was a cheeky git but it got me thinking. Then he said that any goings-on were too gross to imagine and it made me dead ashamed that such a little kid could ask a question like that. I wanted to be a better mother than my mum ever was, but I was a long way off it. Dickie's offer to help me seemed the perfect answer. Little did I know he had other plans for me and my Alfie.

Mummy, I don't think Alfie was pleased to see me at his party... even though it took a lot of arranging so you wouldn't find out... He'd been keen for me to be there and... I thought it was a proper date.

I'm very sleepy Mummy but I need to tell you things...Alfie was different when I got there... He didn't look after me like I thought he would and I didn't know anybody. I didn't...fit in. They were all very...rough. And they stared at me as if I was an alien. And then a boy, well, a man really, came up and offered me a cigarette... I said no thanks but he placed it between my lips and said, 'chill little girl. Take a puff of this and you'll feel great.'

Lottie

Tom wasn't best pleased when I told him about my visit to the illustrious Nancy; he looked seriously annoyed and I caught a flash of disappointment. But eventually he laughed.

'I can just imagine the scene Snooks. I wonder if Dr Nancy Edmunds was ready for Lottie Hanson!' He chuckled so much even I could see the funny side. 'Oh Snooks, you need to give it a least one more try. Nancy comes with tip-top credentials.' So in his usual Tom-like way, he persuaded me to ring and apologise and have another go. I made an appointment for the following week although I had no idea what it would achieve.

The days slipped by in abject misery. Guilt built up over the late starts every morning and I found it hard to focus on anything without Saskia around. I missed her unladylike habit of whistling which drove Tom wild, but I would have given anything to hear her whistle, just once. She'd started raiding my wardrobe for clothes before she went to that ghastly party. She 'borrowed' things that weren't considered 'too Mumsie' and that included my precious L'eau de Issey perfume. She'd become obsessed with her appearance and Mum told me it was quite normal for a girl of sixteen. But all I could remember was wearing jeans and helping Dad with the cows at that age, and I certainly wasn't chasing boys. How things change.

I remember my inactivity was beginning to make me feel old and useless. Too often I heart-searched and found countless flaws in my ability to mother a child. After we'd been gifted our daughter, I let her get stabbed and mixed up with drugs. That snagged at my heart especially as we were so close and I thought she could confide in me. Endless negatives ran on a continuous loop in my brain and drove me insane with guilt. I thought I understood Saskia's every heartbeat, but realised I'd deluded myself.

When I thought about the weeks leading up to the party I had to admit she'd been a little distant, but I'd put it down to hormones; everyone told me it was normal for a sixteen year old girl to be secretive. As my experience of child care was limited to boys who were simple enough, I took advice and let her work through whatever was happening inside her head. Only it wasn't happening inside her head was it? With hindsight, I knew why she hadn't been communicating with us and that yob Alfie Collins had a lot to answer for. He'd driven a mechanical shovel through my very being.

I felt wretched. My hair was caught back in a fat sleeping plait and I looked about seventy. Grey hairs were prominently intermingled with the red and I knew, in another life, it would be time to start colouring them. But not at the moment. I hadn't even washed it for a week.

I heard Enid, my daily, bumping around the kitchen. Tom was long-gone and although I was full of good intent to get up and have breakfast with him one morning, it obviously wasn't on the agenda that day.

I showered and made it to the kitchen but didn't fancy any breakfast.

'Morning Mrs Hanson. It's nice to see you up.'

From anyone else it would have sounded like sarcasm, but not from Enid. She was the most loyal person I knew and was already hard at it on her knees, fumbling under the dresser with dexterity no woman her age should possess. I winced as I thought about her knees on the lime-stone tiles, but she was oblivious.

'Good Morning Enid. I'm up but not sure I'm functioning.'

'Baby-steps. That's what you need. Baby-steps. Good job those boys are off home for half term. Give you a bit of a rest.'

'You're right,' I appeased her. 'But we've had to cancel our holiday in Scilly. Everything is so... uncertain.' I felt the tears welling. 'It'll be the first year Saskia's missed her beach holiday since she was two.'

'You can make up for it when she's better. She'll love a little holiday when she wakes.' She dived to clean a mark off the floor. I knew she struggled to manage our family's trauma, almost as much as we did.

I pondered her wisdom and wondered if we would ever watch Penzance disappear on the horizon as we sailed to our haven that was Scilly. How far away it felt. I struggled to recall the sensation of feet on powdery sand and I couldn't smell the golden narcissi that defined the islands in winter.

'I picked your cream skirt up from the dry-cleaners on my way in. It's still got a stain right on the front.' Enid rose from her knees, gaining purchase on the kitchen table before she leaned her ample body across it. 'I'll take it back when I go home and they can do it again. For free.' She pushed her glasses up her nose.

We were so lucky to have Enid working for us. She was devoted to Tom and Saskia and I reaped the benefits of her kindness, too. She'd been a backbone to the family since...well, for ever it seemed, but especially while Saskia was in hospital.

'Thanks for that'. I didn't care a jot about my cream skirt. I couldn't even remember when I'd last worn it. Dear Enid. She tried her best to keep body and soul together for us.

'Shall I.......' Enid hesitated and I knew what was coming...... 'give the pink room a do?'

'Not today Enid.' I was sharper than she deserved but it was the best I could do. No one would touch Saskia's room until I was ready. I still needed to spend time there. I liked to hug her collection of fluffy dogs and her darling Casper Bear and I knew he'd be the first thing she'd want when she woke. Everything was just where she'd left it, pristine and colour-co-ordinated. My daughter had a very precise eye about such things which she certainly didn't get from me. More likely from...but who knew where an adopted child got their traits? If it's from nurture then Tom took the credit - my scatty lifestyle drove him nuts at times.

'Not today, thanks. I'll put coffee on and I'll call when it's ready.' I couldn't imagine a day when I'd say, *'Enid, give my daughter's room a good spring clean, would you? Bundle up her clothes and I'll pop them down to the charity shop.'* I had to believe she'd come home. I knew all the text book stuff about moving on at my own pace, and I knew there were no rights or wrongs for dealing with trauma because I had a master's degree in counsellor speak. But no one would violate Saskia's room which was waiting for her to come home. I told her every time I visited and always gave her an update on Casper.

I nibbled on a piece of toast and noticed the view through the Victorian sash windows was, as always, stunning. No matter what time of year, it was always beautiful and I was filled with gratitude for the lifestyle I'd adopted. I never tired of those Wimbledon-perfect lawns and the brimming, colour-laden borders. That summer they were themed in blues and lavenders and were heart achingly lovely, although I realised I hadn't noticed them as often as I should over the past few weeks. In fact, I was ashamed to admit I hadn't achieved anything over the previous few weeks. The catastrophe with Saskia had created a maelstrom of hurt that was raw and smarting and never seemed to draw breath; that was on the good days. On bad days I felt like I was bleeding inside. Those were the days when a physical pain enveloped me; those were the duck down days. But I found the not knowing what the future held was the real killer. Not knowing if she would ever be our old Saskia again.

Day after miserable day I dissected our parenting skills, or lack of them, which filled many hours with misgivings. Our first mistake, I decided, was giving Saskia our complete trust and I hated to think it, but were we both too busy with the boys and the business of term-time to notice what she was up to? Tom was forgiven as he had a massive work load at school, but me, I should have known something was going on. There was no excuse for me and I knew I'd never forgive myself.

I put the coffee on to perk and stared out of the window, wondering if concentration on something beautiful might change our lives. It had been a long and tedious road to get to the point of having a child, and now I'd thrown her away. I felt such an idiot. After all our efforts to have her, I'd let her slip through my fingers.

Tom and I spent years on the 'baby treadmill,' trying to produce a longed for baby until we finally conceded defeat. 'Sometimes there's no good reason why you can't conceive,' the best physician known to man told us, all those years ago. 'You're both healthy individuals but it just isn't happening for you.' Cold comfort was how I viewed his wisdom. And, if I'm honest, we were tired of making love to order. Following temperature charts and checking dates took all the spontaneity out of our sex life.

We had several unsuccessful attempts at IVF which cost a fortune, but more importantly, left me feeling like a pin cushion packed with useless hormones. Tom, for whatever reason, felt less than the man he wanted to be. It surprised me that trying to get pregnant could become such a burden, especially as friends were dropping babies as easily as peeling grapes. I thought I'd have an emotional melt-down if another friend asked us to be godparents to their new arrival. Eventually, we gave up the fight and faced the monumental process of adoption.

It took months and months of parent training classes and the indignity of strangers delving into our intimate lives before a tussle headed, two year old became 'available for adoption'. Issues were raised about Saskia's first two years of life with her birth family. The social worker explained they ranged from child neglect to questions about sexual interference, all of which I preferred to bury deeper than Tutankhamun's tomb. Considering her difficult start in life, it was a miracle she'd grown into such a competent, charming and beautiful young woman and it filled my heart to bursting. When I thought of her lying in a coma, it filled my heart so full of tears, I feared it would break.

We brought Saskia to Churchill's when she was two. The finalising of her adoption coincided with Tom's promotion to house master at Churchill's, which felt like the icing on the cake. After long years spent in the desert of childlessness, it was the most exciting and perfect time in our marriage.

Having Saskia helped me settle into our new life. There were plenty of mothers with children on the Churchill campus, many ensconced there by ambitious husbands striving to excel in their profession. For many years I'd avoided women with children to stave off the heartache, but it felt different when Saskia arrived - I felt as if I fitted in and I found friendship too. But for Tom, who was living and working in his alma mater, life continued to rotate on a solid axis.

Saskia was a cheeky, red-headed little angel with freckles and a cute smile and she enchanted us like nothing had before. Tom and I were obsessed with her. We checked her in the middle of the night to be sure she was breathing and she wasn't allowed near a nut for fear of allergy. Her arrival thrilled Mum and Dad too and I was almost as happy for them as I was for us.

I wanted to spend as much time as possible at the hospital with our daughter, watching her while she slept and Tom tipped up at every spare minute he had. I took fresh clothes for her and a bundle of optimism each time I visited. I even took the perfume we'd given at Christmas because a nurse told us scent could be evocative and we were desperate to give anything a try. I used to paint her nails too, usually something soft and pink to match her dress or deep red when I dressed her in leggings. I wanted her to look her best when she woke because she'd never have forgiven me if I'd allowed her to become a mess while she slept. How Saskia looked was paramount to her day and I wasn't going to be found wanting in that department.

I talked to her and held her hand while she slept. 'She may be able to hear you,' the doctor told us when she was admitted. 'Talk to her as if she's awake. No one knows for sure what she hears.' So I told her how much she was loved. I told her that we weren't cross with her, even though we were. I told her how well her tummy had healed but I didn't tell her about the ugly scar the knife had left in her abdomen. And I told her to wake up so that we could take her home.

I suddenly noticed the coffee was ready and I called to Enid. The pungent waft under my nose urged me to action and I poured a large mug for me and a smaller one for Enid who was caffeine conscious. Buck up Lottie Hanson, I told myself. Enough self-pity.

'Shall I boil you an egg Mrs Hanson? Nice and soft, just the way you like 'em?'

'No thanks Enid. Coffee will do for now. Don't let yours get cold.

'I'll just empty the bin. Give it time to cool down.' She chuckled in her inimitable way. 'I looked in the fridge,' she told me as she shook out a new bin-liner. 'Seems like there's a bit of... out-of-date food in there. Shall I chuck it?'

'Thanks.' I felt a tingle of embarrassment. Wasn't that the sign of a slovenly housewife? We didn't eat much during those dark weeks and I knew Mum would have frowned upon my wastefulness.

We sat in companionable silence until Enid told me she'd decided to spring-clean the sitting room. I was never totally comfortable having a daily help, but Enid was wrapped inside the package of privileges that came as standard for a Housemaster at Churchill's. She came alongside the delivery of wines and spirits we received each term, our family food allowance and our daily newspapers. In addition to Enid, we had an odd-job man and a chef who not only fed the boys, but our family too. It was hard to stay in touch with reality when you lived at Churchill's.

I was staring into the dregs of my coffee which were already cold and could sense the energy expelled by Enid as she moved furniture and hoovered next door. She appeared to have the strength of two men and nothing was ever too menial for her. Jolly Enid's face always suggested she was deeply privileged to clear up other folk's grime and dirt. Scrubbing around our walk-in shower and popping her head down someone's loo could be the highlight of her day. She was avidly loyal to Churchill College and all who sailed in her. And she was kind too. Over the last few weeks she'd knitted Saskia a family of pink rabbits which she thought would match her pink bedroom. 'She'll love 'em Mrs Hanson. You see if she don't?' I secretly thought she'd hate them but I'd ensure Enid's feelings weren't hurt when Saskia woke.

If given the chance, Enid would regale all the departments within Churchill's ancient walls it had been her pleasure to serve. 'Boy's Maid, that's how I started. Loved them I did. 'Specially the new boys. Bless their little hearts. Hardly old enough to tie their shoelaces, let alone come to boarding school. Don't know how their mothers leave 'em here.'

How indeed? I quietly agreed with her on that point but over the years, the sentiment was dumbed down to compliment my roll of House Master's wife. I loved the boys too - some more than others, it had to be said. I'd spent years entertaining a variety of boys to afternoon tea in our home, usually half a dozen at a time. They'd devour my chocolate cake as if they'd not seen food for a week and often I'd arrange a video night to make boarding school feel more like home. Saskia was always to be found in the middle of the fun and she learned at an early age how to manipulate the male of the species. As the boys got older, I taught some of them to cook in our farmhouse-style kitchen. 'It's a great way to impress girls,' I'd tease them. 'If you can throw together a spag bol, you can't fail to impress.'

I usually sat with them after the cooking and joined in their banter as they scoffed the product of their labour. 'An honorary chap', they called me. 'Not like staff and not like mothers.' I liked that a lot and I never regretted the mountain of washing up they created. Every pot and pan would be caked in sauce and strings of cheese clung to my Crown Derby. Never having a son of my own, I'd developed a special rapport with the boys and on more than one occasion, Tom had reason to admonish me for what he pompously called my 'over familiarity.'

'You can't tell them that winning games doesn't matter. Not in this establishment,' he once said after our boys lost the final of the inter-house Rugby Cup.

It all seemed so pointless to me, sending the boys out on wet, freezing cold afternoons to wrestle the hell out of each other in the name of ball games. Who cared who won? But I learned to keep my thoughts to myself and my mouth tightly zipped. Over the years, the fragrance of money and the twang of upper crust England honed me into something resembling a good House Master's wife. I learned to stand on the touch line and call for success of the team in dulcet, lady-like tones.

Enid bumbled into the kitchen which moved me to action. I glanced at the clock and felt ashamed when I saw it was past ten. I should have rung Ursula and asked her over for coffee this week, but I hadn't, I'd been neglectful of my social circle. Friends were supportive about Saskia but none of them understood the pain of talking to an unresponsive daughter who lay with closed eyes. There was never anything to hold on to, nothing to indicate she'd ever come back. Not a flicker showed on her beautiful face and eventually you imagined the worst. How could you not? Tom had forbidden me to look at any more websites about 'continuous vegetative states.' He especially banned me from reading the details about a racing driver who'd been in a coma for years. I was driving myself mad, but friends couldn't be expected to understand.

I noticed my diary on the dresser and realised I was in breach of promise. Nancy asked me to keep a diary and was insistent I should write something in it each day. It would help me measure how things improved – well that was the theory. But most days I had no idea what to write so I didn't write anything. I could have written, *feel like shit...again. Cleaned teeth.* I'm sure Nancy would have considered that a lack of effort on my part, but it was the best I could do.

Mummy, the man who'd been nice to me was suddenly horrid, he wanted...sex. I could feel his hand up my dress and he was fumbling...in my knickers. I was so scared. He had a knife and threatened to cut me if I refused him. I was petrified... He...he pushed me down on a pile of coats put his hand over my mouth - I could hardly breath and was afraid to move. There was someone's black leather jacket near my head. I hated the smell....it reminded me of that goat on Bryher, the one we took photos of in the telephone box. Do you remember? I wanted to take it home and then I cried when Daddy said I couldn't. What a spoilt little kid I was. But I'm not a kid now and I got myself into a real pickle at Alfie's party. Now I can't find a way back to you and Daddy.

I put my coffee mug in the dishwasher. I could see boys playing rugby in Nether Field which adjoined the far corner of our garden. Their voices filtered across the lawns, 'Pass it. Pass it here!' In many ways, the boys at Churchill's quelled my longing to have more children of my own. I'd have loved a houseful if they had come our way, but it wasn't to be and we learned to be satisfied with our beautiful daughter. Optimistic people told us that after adopting a child, hormones often kicked in and pregnancy could follow. But it wasn't to be for us.

Over the years the ache for more babies calmed itself. I became a realist and threw myself into my role as Tom's support which taught me to applaud every success of the boys in our house and smile with delight as I presented trophies to the talented. And I learned to be amusing and witty when asked to host dinner parties or entertain parents. Most of all, I made my own parents proud. Dad told anyone who'd listen about his successful daughter and her *life with the nobs*. Bet that went down well at Cirencester cattle market!

Enid appeared and plonked her backside on a kitchen chair. She put her feather duster on the table. 'The Boy's Maids are on the warpath,' she announced.

'Oh. Is it something Tom should know about?'

'No. It's to do with dirty pants under beds. They seems to be hoarding them for some reason.'

'It's not the first time. I'll bet Galbraith is one of them. He's such a dirty boy.'

There was a time when I thought Galbraith was summoning up courage to ask Saskia to the cinema. When I mentioned it to Saskia and teased a little she asked if I thought he'd scrub himself up a bit beforehand. I knew she'd turned him down and I wished things could have been different.

'You'd think they had to do their own washing instead of sticking everything in a laundry bag,' Enid vented.

'I'll have a word. See if prohibiting their Saturday treats does the trick.'

'Reckon it will. Never seen kids stuff so many sweet as this lot.'

Enid wandered off to more cleaning after turning Tom's radio from Radio Four to something offering music she could sing along to. I smiled despite my misery. How did she stay so cheerful?

Tracey

I never clocked it for ages but Dickie started giving money to Alfie; I first noticed it around Alfie's fourteenth birthday when a crisp fiver was shoved under the teapot like it had a purpose. I thought it was a present from old Dickie. What I never knew was what went on after I left for work that day.

'There's a little job I need doing', Old Dickie told him when he saw Alfie clock the note.

'Oh yeh? Legs can't get you to the shop to buy your own ciggies I 'spose?' (he had a right gob on him, my Alfie.)

'No..... it's nothing as simple as that'......

'Spit it out then. A fiver would be better in my pocket than yours, Old Man'.

'Less of your lip, Nipper. That's if you want to get yerself a regular little earner'.

'I ain't got all day, Dickie'.

'Well, it's a bit delicate.' Dickie gave his nose a conniving tap. 'Sort of...man-stuff. Think you're up to man's stuff? Keep yer gob shut can yer'?

'Try me'.

I'd have rung Dickie's scrawny neck if I'd heard the dirty old man talking to my Alfie like that.

Alfie first started his antics when he was about ten. It was just throwing stones at the empty factory off Claymore Street to begin with. A gang of them used to hop over the wall where the topping stones had slipped and once inside the compound they'd take bets on who could smash the most windows with bricks they found lying around the site. Around the same time, he took up with some older boys who used to nick petrol out of cars. At first he just stood lookout; he told me he used to keep an eye out for the fuzz. After a bit, they let him try his hand and told him to suck on the plastic pipe they'd dropped into the tank of an old, beat-up van. What they didn't tell him was that he had to stop sucking just before the fuel hit his throat; it was nothing to them but my Alfie nearly choked to death. They laughed their socks off, apparently. It was a bit like giving a blow-job, he told me years later. After that, I think the gang decided to promote him and he became a little thug who was afraid of nothing and no one.

I was furious that Old Dickie had the nerve to grubby my boy. But what could I do? Dickie had me back on the game and I earned so much more money than at the shop. I needed it from somewhere 'cos two kids cost the earth to feed and clothe. I know I should've gone to the Social but I was ....sort of in it before I knew it and Dickie always told me they'd take my kids away if I dobbed him in. My Alfie was fourteen and should have been playing football not taking filthy money from Dickie. That's prostitution of the worst kind in my book. Using kids. But my Alfie loved it 'cos he'd never had so much money in his life. It was more than I ever seemed to have. And that's how Alfie got away from me; he never needed anything from me after that.

Alfie was always going on about who his dad was when he was at school. 'Load of good for nothing', I told him when he asked. 'Not worth the shirt he stood up in'. Well, he'd have liked to have been the judge of that, he said. Obviously, he knew his dad must be some shade of brown, he knew that by just by looking in the mirror. He used to tell me, 'I don't care if he's a wanker, at least he'll be *my* wanker if you tell me who it is.' It was heart breaking. How could I tell him his dad was knifed to death in prison ten years before? He had so much hope in those brown eyes that I didn't have the heart to tell him.

'Does he live round here then?'

'No'.

'How did you meet him then?'

'Never you mind'.

He told me that sometimes he'd pretend the school bus driver was his Dad. He'd imagine waiting 'til all the kids got off the bus and then he'd say, 'Oy mate, I'm yer kid'. He'd have liked a dad who was a bus driver. Actually, I used to think anybody real would do. Well, anybody except a copper. Couldn't imagine having a dad who turned out to be a copper, could he? He'd been picked up by the fuzz more times than I could remember. But Alfie made no headway with me and eventually stopped asking.

When he got the hang of girls, Alfie told me he didn't think it was all it was cracked up to be. The local girls were mostly slappers who were hell bent on getting pregnant to get a council flat. They'd think nothing of dropping their pants before leaning on the wall behind the youth club. I knew 'cos I'd been one of them. That's how Alfie came along and I had to leave school to have him. But I'd tried to make Alfie want more than that. He always said he didn't want to be tied down with a slapper and a kid and I hoped he meant it. Not that I thought he'd get it on with a girl from that posh college. Her mother should have known better than to let her loose on my Alfie. Enough to turn a boy's head, wasn't it?

Alfie used to tell me snippets of what went on with the street gangs, if he was in a good mood.

'How do you know when a Murton slag has an orgasm? She drops her pasty!'

Alfie said the lads never failed to find that one funny. The Murton Estate was full of 'quick fix girls' and my Alfie soon got bored with them. But then he found a posh girl and ended up in bloody prison. He'd have been better tied with a Murton slag and a kid, than in prison.

When he was coming up eighteen my Alfie had a chance to make something of his life, or so I thought, at first. The volunteer do-gooder at the youth club fell over the fact that he could slap a bit of paint on a canvas. I don't think Alfie cut her much slack to begin with, but she kept admiring what she called his 'free spirit with a brush' until she won him over. The winning-over was little more than an exchange of a few words from what I could gather. The do-gooder encouraged him and arranged for him to work in the local posh college art room. It was only once a week to start with, but I noticed he started going more often. He couldn't go in if la-de-da parents were visiting nor during exam periods, other than that he could go pretty much when he liked as long as he signed the visitor's book and marked himself out when he left.

I met the twit of a volunteer who arranged it one day while I was shopping in Lidle's and she told me 'Alfie has blossomed within the hallowed walls of Churchill's College.' 'Blossomed' my ass. I just thought that while he was sitting in upper-crust England, he needed to remember it was only four short miles from Skankland. We both knew that the only reason he was allowed in was to do with the Government's idea of *'giving the under-class a bit of a go'*, but he seemed to like it and I hoped he would change his lifestyle. He was definitely seeing less of the hoodlums but, of course, it turned out he was shagging that girl.

Alfie told me the college boys all thought his art was good. If he was in a good mood he'd sit with a cup of coffee and tell me all about it. He could take-off their plummy accents like he was born to it and used to make me laugh 'til I cried. I could never imagine him in that school, not in a month of Sundays. But he liked people thinking he was talented; he liked the fact they found some good in him. Who wouldn't like a bit of praise now and then? Especially as he wasn't used to it. He told me about one college lad who wasn't a stuck up little prick. Toby, he was called and he painted similar stuff to Alfie.

'You're really good', Toby told him without a bite of sarcasm. 'I wish I could capture that raw, street-quality.'

'I live it. That's why it looks real. Thing is, I can't imagine having an Old Man who earned enough to send me here.'

'I can't imagine having all that freedom either. Can you really stay out all night without having to tell your Mum? Doesn't she worry?'

'Naw. She knows I can look out for myself'

But did I? Broke me heart when he told me things like that. Brought home what a lousy mother I'd been.

I must 'ave slept a bit in Alfie's bed but me head was still throbbing. I got out real slow and took a gander at what Alfie called his 'portfolios.' I suppose I was curious. I didn't usually take any interest but maybe I should have. His massive paintings were propped against the walls and the canvas alone probably cost more than our week's grocery, even without his 'artistic contribution' as he liked to call it. Huge splashes of vivid, angry colours, more like kindergarten work than done by an eighteen year old, supposedly 'talented man.' He liked to think he was a man, although to me he was still just a kid. He was a kid with a chip on his shoulders big enough to sink the bleeding Titanic.

My Lily always came out of school like a ray of sunshine. She loved learning. I knew she'd notice me bruises and I'd have to tell her I fell 'cos she was still young enough to swallow small lies. I needed to tell her about Alfie, too. Luckily she was at school when they arrested him but she'd already asked why he wasn't home. We were used to him disappearing for a few days, but this was a bit too long. I was surprised no one had told her at school, really so I decided to tell her when we had tea. I bought two big sticky buns 'cos she loved them and I hoped it would soften the blow when she heard about her big brother. She asked if she could stay home the next day after I told her, but she went to school as usual and hardly mentioned it again.

I sometimes thought all Alfie's problems started when Lily was born. He was nine at the time and I guessed he was jealous. One day I caught him nearly throttling her and he said, 'I'm just loving her Mum. She'll laugh in a minute.' I knew to be a bit more careful after that.

He took to going out without telling me where he was going. Old Dickie brought him home on more than one occasion with tales of all the scrapes he'd got into. In fact, it was through Alfie that I got to know Old Dickie. I thought he was just a lonely old man, really. He had no family that he ever spoke about and was often happy to baby sit while I made a few extra quid in the evenings. The corner shop was always looking for people to put in some hours at night and I had a few regulars back in them days, too. Mum had known Dickie for years and she said she thought he was OK to leave with the kids.

When I was growing up I'd heard people say 'there's no such thing as a free lunch' and that one came home to roost soon after old Dickie appeared on the scene. After about two months of getting to know him, it started with, 'let me put the kettle on love, you look parched.' He'd sit me down like I was the Queen and make me a nice cup of tea, more often than not with a Hobnob to dunk. 'A bit of sympathy goes a long way', I'd heard Mum mention more than once and Old Dickie was good at tea and sympathy. To be honest, I didn't really notice him wheedling his way in, but before I knew it I had a door key cut and he was popping in just when he was needed, and often when he wasn't.

Alfie was a latch key kid but I wanted better for Lily. Leaving the key on a piece of string through the letterbox wasn't safe and I'd promised myself I'd try to be home when school finished. Sometimes I made her a jam sandwich or even a bit of home-made cake. I was learning all the time.

I had to admit Old Dickie turned out to be a God-send. If I couldn't meet Lily from school then he was the next best thing and Lily liked him. He seemed OK with her so it worked for all of us. Not that she was a difficult kid. Not like Alfie. Lily worked hard at school and she could read when she was five. She always wanted to please, which saved one hell of a lot of grief, especially after bringing up Alfie.

Thinking back, it was probably just the odd touch in a doorway that started it. A sort of 'sorry' as Old Dickie brushed past me while going through gaps. But it soon became obvious that it was deliberate. I could have told Mum but thought she'd over-react and face him up about it. Then I'd have no sitter for Lily 'cos Mum wouldn't give up her comings and goings to babysit for me.

He was old enough to be me grandfather. God that sounded bleak when you put it like that. I preferred to think we were both needy. You know, both needing somebody for a bit of a cuddle. I asked meself what difference age made anyway. He wasn't revolting. Just old. In need of a good steam iron when he took his clothes off but, hey, beggars couldn't be choosers back then.

I never thought of myself as lovable, I never had the looks. But if some lonely old man who liked my kids wanted to give me a quick shag now and then, where was the harm in that? It *was* a quick shag, too.

One day he showed me a picture of himself in some sort of soldiers' uniform taken when he was about twenty. National Service, he said, whatever that was. After that I found it helped the shags along a bit if I pictured him during his better days. Quite handsome he was. Passed the time when I imagined him in his hey-day, as he called it. 'All the girls fell over themselves to go dancing with me,' he told me, 'right light on me feet I was.'

But he wasn't very bloody light on his feet when I knew him, though I got used to his finger-wagging routine to coax me onto his lap. I'd have liked a dad who did that. Just for a cuddle. I wanted one who read me stories at bedtime and felt all whiskery. But after I sat on Dickie's lap for a while, he'd heave his arthritic joints out of the chair and take me along to the bedroom where he'd collapse with a groan onto his back. 'Spose he was lucky to still get it up at his age, but it isn't exactly 'a cake with a cherry on the top', as Mum would have said. I got good at it and in fairness, it never took long. He was a noisy bugger 'tho, and more than once I had to slap his Y fronts over his mouth to shut him up in case of nosy neighbours. I hated gossip from the neighbours.

I remember I'd been trying to save up to take Lily to the Zoo. She loved animals and I'd been promising for ages that we'd go. I was still short by quite a few quid when Dickie said, 'have a few quid from me, it's just a little something to help get you there this side of Christmas.' Cheeky sod, I thought 'cos I was funny like that. I never liked to take charity off no one. But he'd said it in front of Lily, so what could I do? And we had a cracking day out. I even squeezed a cheap tea out of the money as well. Lily was well happy.

Soon after that, came what Dickie called a 'business proposition'. It went something like this; 'everybody has something they're good at and you, my little pigeon pie are a bloody good shag. If you've got a talent then you should use it to make a bob or two'. He'd got it all worked out. He'd be in my flat with Lily while I used his old people's flat or 'Sheltered Housing' as he liked to call it at Skankland. I'd be doing what I was 'good at' and sharing the money with a man old enough to be my grandfather. 'No one would suspect', he convinced me. 'Who would think you were carrying-on in sheltered housing? They'd think you're in there doing a bit of cleaning.' At least it would be safe, I thought and my hours at the corner shop had just been cut. Money was tight as hell and I wanted my Lily to have everything I never had. Mondays and Thursdays the 'arrangement' was gonna be at first, with men supplied by Old Dickie. 'They better be clean,' I told him. 'And none of that kinky stuff.'

Mummy, I'm still trying, honest I am... but I can't wake up. I keep thinking about that horrible man and why didn't Alfie do more? I know I screamed a lot but... I was so frightened the knife would slip. He held the knife and...it was touching the skin on my throat and his other hand was inside my knickers. I remember thinking... he couldn't...you know...get inside me with only one hand free.

Lottie

The trips to hospital were difficult; every single day we mustered courage to face the barrage of medical equipment that beeped, ticked and seeped fluid in and out of Saskia's body. It was an unnatural world. It was hard and clinical but somewhere amongst it all, was my daughter. For Tom and me, life was full of conflict. Every visit was a reminder of that bastard's violation of our precious girl as we came face to face with the damage he'd inflicted on her perfect body. And yet seeing her also eased the heartache, if only for a short while. Caring for the bodily needs of my sleeping daughter was the only practical thing I could offer. I fed her through a tube and watched as the milky fluid disappeared to nourish her from within. I washed and changed her as if she was a baby again, only now she had none of the feistiness of her infant self. I longed for her to tell me her nail polish was the wrong colour or she hated to wear trousers. And yet in my heart I knew it may never happen and our lives were charged with conflict and contradiction. Being near her had that amniotic pull all mothers feel and I stared deeply into her pretty face and prayed for a sign of change. I made deals with God. I held her hands which were warm and living and felt just like our old Saskia. But she wasn't there, was she?

When we were a few weeks into the trauma I had almost come to terms with that life-changing night when Saskia slipped out of our sight full of lust and deceit. I'd probably even come to terms with the logistics of how she did it. All the sneaking about and the lies were in the past and no matter how much I wanted to change it, I couldn't. By now, above anything, I wanted her back home. I wanted our lovely daughter to open her eyes, I wanted to hear her speak and I wanted assurance that she wasn't brain damaged. I reasoned, if Saskia had lost the use of her legs, I'd have spent every waking hour helping her to walk again. I'd have driven her on to greater achievement. And I'd have believed she could do it. But this! This was in a different league. Day after day there was no sign of improvement. There was nothing. No sign, real or imagined told us Saskia was still inside her body.

If getting up in the morning was an achievement, then I made progress. I wrote in the famous diary and gave myself a pat on the back for small achievements. 'Have a plan for the day, however small. Have a reason to get up,' were the words of wisdom from clever Nancy. Saskia was my *raison d'etre.*. I knew all the theory of dealing with the tragedy but I struggled to put it into practice. How the hell Tom managed to get up each morning to deal with the demands of adolescent boys was beyond me. I knew it was unreasonable to be angry with him. But my anger had a habit of firing pellets at those I loved best. Some days I accused Tom of not feeling the pain that crippled me both night and day; I knew that was spiteful but it was just me lashing out at the nearest and dearest. I think I'd harboured some unreasonable fear that I might lose him, too. Anxiety lurked in my peripheral vision every time we were apart. He could have fallen under a bus or got himself mugged by a drug-crazed youth with a knife. It was those words that echoed like a mantra.

My pathetic lack of confidence felt like my alter ego. I was unfamiliar with being a wimp and it was hard to find any normality in my life. But how *could* life be normal without Saskia? 'Men cope differently,' the clever, perfect counsellor told me with monotonous regularity. 'They feel things in a different way and getting back to work is a coping mechanism.' Yeh, right. Maybe I needed some of that.

I sometimes played the '*what if*' game. It was pointless, but I had so much time on my hands. '*What if,*' Tom had chosen a grammar school for his teaching career instead of this snooty public school? *'What if,'* we weren't living in a goldfish bowl, (or rather, a cut glass champagne flute?) *'What if,'* our family life wasn't planted in the echelons of money and power? If Tom had chosen a teaching job in a comprehensive school we'd have lived in a normal house, had normal friends and never had to deal with this. Tom would have come home every evening around five carrying bundles of marking, asking what's for supper and checking on Saskia's homework. So it must be Tom's fault then. But it was too easy to lay blame and I tried harder not to play that blame game. But some days I hardly spoke to my husband and I could feel that we were poles apart. But when I reflected on our lives, I had to be honest and admit, I too had learnt to enjoy the cloistered environment of public school life. The privilege of money and education had undoubtedly softened both of us and I appreciated that we lived an extraordinary life.

An unimaginable burden was dumped on Tom ten years after we were married when his elder brother died in a car accident. It devastated the family. And as if losing your big brother wasn't enough, he also lost his best buddy who was heir to the family estate and title. As second born son, Tom had been shooed into the world to make his own way, but suddenly, amidst all the sadness, he was expected to put aside his loathing for the estate and pick up the responsibilities. There was another life waiting in the wings and like the sword of Damocles, it threatened our happiness.

Amidst all the shock and sorrow I assumed Tom's dream of a teaching career was over and steeled myself for the inevitable lifestyle change. But Tom surprised me and I was full of admiration for his grit and single-mindedness at the time. He stamped his foot firmly on the soil of inheritance and money, and announced he wasn't up for the responsibility of the estate and certainly not the care of his ailing mother

'Piers knew I never wanted the estate. He always encouraged me to follow my own career,' he told his mother. This I knew to be correct but circumstances had taken such an acute turn that I feared family honour would melt Tom's resolve. But it didn't.

After long days of heart searching and misery, and after a gut-wrenching funeral to lay his brother to rest in the family crypt, Tom risked the wrath of his mother by declining to step into his brother's shoes. The title came to Tom regardless of any decisions he made, but he vowed never to use it. The Cotswold pile and three hundred acres of land with its corresponding overheads, was also Tom's.

But his mother was the biggest deciding factor when choosing to follow his own career, as neither of us could envisage running the estate while she was alive. The Old Dame, as I called my mother-in-law from hell, had never accepted her second son's decision to teach at Churchill's. I once heard her mutter, 'we didn't spend all that money on your education for you to become *just* a teacher. And why on earth did you marry a girl from nothing?' She really was a ghastly old lady. 'Her head's up her ass,' as my dad so daintily put it.

It was agreed after much posturing from his mother, that a cousin would run the estate until such time as Tom 'came to his senses'.

Tom was passionate about educating young minds and spurring on successful teenagers. His heart was patently in teaching. When he took his first class honours degree to his alma mater and began his career as a humble classroom teacher, he knew he'd found his niche in life.

But I wasn't exactly a duck to water on the matter. As much as I wanted Tom to be happy, I had a career of my own I wanted to follow and found it hard to acquiesce. He surely found my hypothetical kicking and screaming hard to deal with as I didn't want to live amongst wealth and power. The feisty girl I was then made sure he knew it. For one thing, it stood in the way of my hopes to make my parents proud of me. I was going to be the space scientist that changed the world. I'd spent a few years in engineering heaven with a company in Oxford who were involved in space programmes and I'd been offered an opportunity to go to America for some hands-on experience just when Tom popped the question. I loved him and being his wife was worth sacrificing my career, or so I thought at the time.

Part of the package at Churchill's was a perfect little cottage within the grounds and after I took Mum's homely advice which was something along the lines of following where your husband led, I set out to make a success of my new life. But making house and supporting my husband in an alien world was tough. We were newly married and enjoyed cosy evenings eating delicious food and drinking copious amounts of merlot. And we made love with the vigour of youth and with the hope of starting a family. The long school holidays were an added bonus and we travelled to foreign lands but also spent happy times with my parents in the Cotswolds. Tom had never known a real family and I set about encouraging him to share mine.

I was thrown off-kilter by the opulence of Churchill's College and awed by the grandeur and ceremony which everyone but me took for granted. As new arrivals, we were dragged around drinks parties and shown off at raucous dinners. I always felt we were being scrutinised and judged, and many years later, when my feet were well imbedded in the hallowed ground, I knew this to be true. It was for that reason I always made an effort to put new staff at their ease and never forgot my own baptism by fire. But we obviously passed muster as eventually, Tom was offered the post of Housemaster and we plonked ourselves into an entirely new adventure. The house was large enough to contain fifty boys and had a stunning apartment for us which laid claim to the garden side of the house.

I came to realise that this was the life Tom had been raised to and I loved him enough to grasp it and claim it as my own. I settled and eventually became happy with my lot.

And at times I positively loved it although I didn't love anything about life after we lost Saskia. Then, I roamed around in a tepid wash of nothingness. It was like swimming in a sink of cold, greasy washing-up water and there was no point to my days. Each week seemed like a year. I asked myself if I would always gaze at teenagers in the street, seeking out Saskia's sea-green eyes. Would stunning red hair under a shaft of sunlight always make my heart skip a beat? And for how long would I steal into College Chapel and kneel in prayer as if I believed in a higher God? Was it an example of what the clever counsellor called a 'coping mechanism?' Maybe I'd started coping without knowing. That was a bright thought for the day. Get it in the bloody diary!

Our life-style was unusual by most peoples' standards. To begin with, we shared our daily routine with the twelve hundred school boys of Churchill's College. Here, princes and titles were as common as frogspawn in the boating lake. For two thirds of every year our family lived under the same roof as fifty one of the little darlings. I knew their smell, their dirty little ways and their vulnerabilities. Being a Housemaster's wife could be tricky, although I believe I shaped up pretty well; until I had to cope with our life-changing event. Then I was as much use to Tom as a stick of liquorice.

Saskia's coma affected the boys too. They were so sweet when they knocked on our apartment door and brought gifts for her. I hadn't the heart to tell them nothing would go to the hospital until she woke up. Tom said, 'let's keep everything in her room until she comes home, then she'll know how much she was missed.' Luckily, Tom had an excellent house matron who had boundless energy and she picked up many of my little jobs and never stopped smiling. I liked her and was grateful for her support.

Privacy in our personal life during term time was defined by an exhausted half hour chat in bed at night and, before we lost Saskia, a chat over a cup of morning tea. While dealing with the trauma, I can't pretend I didn't sometimes wish I was a million miles away from the precious, opulent life-style that sucks in the gullible and impersonates real life. I had days when I wanted to run home to my parents, to be a child again, to be cared for and have no responsibilities. But the reality was that my lovely parents had no idea how to help. My best friend Fiona in Australia offered to fly over when she heard about Saskia. But I didn't think even she could help. We were lifelong friends and understood each other like sisters. I'd have given anything for her to wrap her arms around me but she was busy with four kids and a sheep rancher husband. I couldn't drag her all that way just to see me blub like a baby over her alpaca jumper.

I had friends in college, too. There was a handful of wives and daughters of the establishment who were somewhere on my wavelength. They tried to be kind and called me regularly for updates, but this was something Tom and I had to bear together. We were too exhausted to have meaningful talks about coma and loss and the division between us widened.

I stopped day dreaming, got myself dressed and decided against using the hot brush. I made a hair appointment instead. Maybe things were looking up at last and I jotted a sentence to that affect in the diary. I looked at the kitchen notice board hanging above the toaster and then wished I hadn't. 'The Bursar invites you.' Oh God. I mused over the sub text; the dinosaur's pad calls you to mingle with a dozen or so sparkling members of Churchill's College for the dreaded drinks party. And it was that evening. I decided to visit Saskia and try to muster the courage to go with Tom to the drinks party. He'd done so much on his own and I knew he'd appreciate the effort if I went with him.

I felt sick. It must have been the vodka I drank. It made me feel very grown up. Smoking the man's cigarette. I'm sorry Mummy...I knew it was some kind of drug but I felt lonely

46

and different. I just wanted to blend into the background and hoped Alfie would talk to me if I wasn't different. Wow the vodka was strong! There weren't any mixers or ice. It was neat and warm and not very nice, actually... But I drank it anyway.

Most days I helped with Saskia's personal care. I washed her and learnt from the nurses how to keep her mouth clean. I moisturised her skin with my best Chanel hand cream and brushed her hair which still held its lustre despite her sleeping state. I bought a dry shampoo which gave better results than I expected. And her nails grew. I'm not sure why that surprised me, but it did. How could life go on as normal? She'd lost weight and hadn't had a period since it happened, but the nurses told me neither was unusual. 'Trauma,' they said. I thought an awful lot was being passed off as 'trauma'. Nothing made sense. I had no idea how those bodily functions related, if at all, to hope for Saskia's future.

The nurses and doctors were friendly and professional and we couldn't have wished for better care for our daughter. But there was no hope of healing for ourselves while she was still damaged. Of course, people grieve differently, but this wasn't grieving, was it? No one can prepare you for the mental tightrope attached to a loved one in a coma; it was like walking on glass or through the fires of hell with no guarantee of reward. And it was Saskia's mental state I had most fears about. Her team told us the CT and MRI scans showed no sign of permanent damage. So why didn't she wake up? And would our exuberant, feisty daughter be a vegetable? The anguish of those words left holes in my heart.

How often I wished I could get my hands on the little shit who'd damaged her; I was sure I'd have squeezed the life from him. I used to lie awake at night and torture myself to the sound of a gently ticking clock that taunted me. I was choked with anger over Alfie Collins and it was eating me alive. What on earth did Saskia see in him? My beautiful girl, who could have had any boy she wanted, had to choose him. I couldn't make sense of it.

Tom told me he met Alfie once in the college Art Room. He explained to me what the lad was doing there and how the art master considered him an excellent artist. Tom even bought one of his bloody paintings, no doubt encouraged by Saskia. At least I had the satisfaction of taking a Stanley knife to that 'so-called art' and shredding it beyond recognition where it hung in her bedroom. It was immensely satisfying at the time, although I recognised it as a childish act.

Tom told me the boy had pale coffee skin, long curly hair and Celtic eyes. Attractive, he said. I tried not to imagine him touching my daughter's perfect body. Did he take her virginity? I couldn't imagine the relationship was a meeting of minds. The doctor said there was no evidence of sexual intercourse that fatal night which had a ring of comfort. We grasped any straw of hope offered.

And of course, there was her deceit to deal with. Mum told me 'it's what teenage kids do. They deceive their parents to get their own way.' Really? But getting herself to that party of hooligans took blatant lies. Planning and lies. God, I was angry. I kept asking myself if she'd thrown away her life on a drug-crazed youth who would hopefully end up in prison for a very long time. But even that wouldn't bring Saskia back to us, would it?

Strangely enough the daytime could be worse than the nights. I seemed to wear a gut-wrenching sense of loss like a second skin during daylight hours. I missed her energy in the house and the fun of being around her. We used to laugh at the most ridiculous things. Saskia could see humour in anything. Often she poked fun at the establishment we lived among and she could mimic the headmaster to a tee. Even Tom was not safe from her wicked humour. I softly admonished her, as a mother should, and then laughed at her very joie de vivre. She stopped me becoming saturated with snooty people and their stuffy traditions. Tom despaired of us. He rarely saw the joke, bless him.

Without Saskia in the house I could barely raise a smile. Every minute of every day I tasted the horror that shrouded our lives; I could smell it when I woke and it knocked on the door like a fox at a hen house; it was never satisfied, always coming back for more. But hey, there were some better days as well when I hovered around a tepid six out of ten for normality. Not bad really.

The police told us a date had been set for the court case. I couldn't believe we would be spending August in court instead of on our beloved Isles of Scilly. Our time out in Scilly was always special but there was no chance we'd walk the Garrison with wind in our hair or dip toes in the freezing, azure waters for the foreseeable future. The future was nothing but a big, fat pile of stress. I agonised about Saskia taking drugs – the real nitty gritty of it. And it was hard to grasp that my baby girl had experienced something even Tom and I had no knowledge of. Did she pop a pill or did she smoke something? Did she know what she was doing or was she forced? When the toxicology report came back, however, we knew she'd taken amphetamines of dubious origin; she'd also smoked pot and drunk a considerable amount of vodka. We were told there had been a spate of problems around the area and the police suspected she had fallen victim to a 'bad batch' which made her coma all the more worrying. And all this would become public knowledge in court and be pounced upon by the press. I think this worried Tom more than it worried me.

Saskia had been given all the drug awareness it was possible to instil in a child. She'd lived with a father who was drug-savvy and vigilante; nothing mattered more to him than to keep the boys in his house safe. Talking about drugs was open and honest and she'd had a no-holds-barred explanation of the perils of taking them. She should have known better; she did know better. She could never claim ignorance of the consequences. But what about the vodka? A huge amount was consumed, we were told. But the worst of it wasn't the drugs or the booze but the knife that ripped her stomach open. Why was she mixing with someone who'd put a knife in her? How could we grasp that concept? Did she refuse him sex? Was sex at the bottom of it all? I drove myself mad, slowly. And then Tom and I had to steel ourselves to sit through the trial.

We both summoned every last strand of courage in readiness to hear Collins talk his way out of what he'd done. Because he intended to plead not guilty, we were forced to face him at trial and where were we supposed to find the strength for that? We also anticipated a plethora of photographers and journalists chasing us, which added to the stress levels. Like bloody leeches, they'd be looking for someone to suck dry. Well I was already desiccated so they'd get no juice from me.

Tracey

I went to see my Alfie and he looked awful. He was pale and thin and all the swagger had gone out of him. At first he sat and stared out the window. Afraid I might try to kiss him I shouldn't wonder. I lied about me bruises and got away with it. But then he looked me in the eyes and all his own troubles tumbled out and it was more than I wanted to hear. Thought I'd ever sleep again. Some of the things he told me…well they shocked even me and I'd been around a bit. Sad little shrimp he looked; he knew he could be facing an eight year stretch but still he said he never done it. Said he didn't give that girl drugs and he didn't knife her. He said she was with an older kid who gate-crashed his party. I asked him who and he said everyone knew him as Zillon. But they'd found Alfie's prints on the knife so that made him a little liar, didn't it?

Apparently the girl was close to death by the time they found her. When the police arrived everyone scarpered, including my Alfie, and the girl was found lying under coats and old curtains. I asked him why he ran if he didn't do nothing but he never answered. Trouble was, all the kids were programmed from a young age to scarper when the fuzz arrived. But that still didn't excuse him for leaving a girl to die. Alfie said he never realised how serious it was. Must have wanted his eyes tested, I told him. He asked if I'd heard how the girl was. 'Saskia Mum. She's called Saskia and I love her'. I didn't know how she was, but I promised I'd ask around. I wanted to change the subject.

'What's it like in here?' I asked him.

'It's shit and likely to get a lot worse. New regulations come in next week,' he told me. 'No more fags allowed, even in our cells. Some of the blokes are going nuts.'

I thought about the consequences of taking away a prisoner's fags. Seemed barbaric to me. My Alfie loved his ciggies and he'd be stuffed without them.

'Poor sods. As if it ain't bad enough in 'ere.'

'They want to give us nicotine patches – like that'll help.'

I told him to give them a try 'cos I knew a couple of people who'd managed to give up on patches. But he wasn't listening. He kept on about his cell. I 'spose that's all he'd seen since he came in.

'I can see where some filthy buggers have spat gob and gum up there. On the ceiling. Looks like the Milky Way if you have a bit of imagination.'

I had to laugh 'cos if there's one thing my Alfie had, it was imagination.

'Only way to pass the time is looking at the ceiling and using yer imagination,' he said which all seemed a bit sad to me. 'Even remand prisoners don't get no perks,' he told me. 'It makes no difference, the rules are the same as if you've been found guilty. And the thing is, I never did it Mum. I might have given Saskia vodka but I never went near any E's and I never stabbed her. I tried to get the knife off the bloke and it went into Saskia instead. I love her. She's the best thing that's happened to me so why would I? But nobody believes me.'

I wondered to myself why that would be. 'Any news on the court case yet?'

'Should be soon. Because I'm remanded I might jump the queue. I cost too much to keep.' He chuckled but I could tell it was false.

I noticed a small boy in the Visiting Hall showing his dad a drawing. It made me heart lurch and took me back a few years to a place I preferred not to remember. Alfie never had that advantage 'cos I refused to bring him inside to see his dad. I started thinking that might have been wrong.

The time went real quick – well it did for me. I had an urge to put my hand over my Alfie's and tell him I'd sort it. Just like when he was a kid. But I couldn't sort it, could I?' After what felt like ten minutes but was actually nearly an hour I looked at Lily's Mickey Mouse watch and realised I'd miss me bus if I didn't go. Alfie let me give him a hug but his body was stiff as a board. I knew he was scared and it broke me heart.

All the way home I tried to come up with a plan to get Alfie out. Why weren't the police looking for this other bloke? Too many questions and no answers did my head in. I felt useless and that's a bad feeling for a mother when her kid's in trouble.

I got off the bus just in time to fetch Lily from school and I needed to tell her I'd been to see her brother. I wanted Lily to have a better chance in life than I'd provided for Alfie. My Lily was bright. She had a real chance to make something of herself, except now she'd got a jail-bird for a brother.

I spotted Mum waiting by the school gate. She was in a leopard print tee-shirt with sparkles that made you wish you was wearing sunglasses and striped trousers that looked like pyjamas. I was embarrassed.

'I told you I'd fetch her.' I was a bit sharp but it don't matter with Mum.

'I know. I wanted to make sure you'd be back.'

'Course I am. Why wouldn't I be?'

'Yeh, why wouldn't you be? Every day yer visit yer son in the nick, I 'spose?'

'Don't need sympathy. Just need everybody to mind their own.'

'I just wanted to 'elp. You know.'

'No, I don't know. Bit late in the day fer motherly concern, don't yer think?

She stomped off muttering about ungrateful kids.

When Lily and me got home Old Dickie was on the doorstep. Spose I should have been pleased he was offering to have Lily while I went to work, but I wanted to smash his face in fer how he'd treated me. I felt full of anger and it was likely to blow.

'Had a fall have you girl?'

I let Lily inside so she wouldn't cotton-on to what he was talking about. I'd told her I bumped into the door and hit my eye.

'A fall, my ass.' He knew exactly what happened to my face or else he'd got a touch of dementia. 'Like you care. You're a bully Dickie and one day...one day my Alfie'll make you pay. You see if he don't.'

'Yeh, yeh. Nothing more than a scratch. That's your trouble. Always have to exaggerate, you do.'

I was livid. I wanted to slam the door in his stupid face and smash his nose. See how he liked it. But I didn't and he followed me indoors.

'I'll put the kettle on and then your little princess can tell me what she's been up to at school.'

Lily smiled like he was Father Christmas. I could have killed her.

I found a biscuit and told Lily to go and tidy her room. Then I turned on Dickie. 'Alfie's going to plead not guilty.' I noticed his weasel face was a bit scrunched like he was thinking. That'd be a first.

'Hmm. Did his brief tell him to do that?'

'No. he says he never done it so he won't plead guilty.'

'Could get less time inside, if he coughs to it.'

'But he's not going to cough if he never done it.'

'Don't look good is what I'm thinking. No witnesses from what I've heard. No witnesses can be as bad as too many. Know what I mean?'

I did know what he meant. It was easier to fit Alfie up than do much digging around. That's what he meant. Tick box exercise for the fuzz.

'Cors, if I could sort out a witness to say Alfie never done it.....well, it would be a whole different ball game, wouldn't it?

I allowed me heart to do a little flip at the thought of Alfie coming home but then I remembered who was holding the carrot and I forgot it. 'Yeh right. Who'd be daft enough to do that then?'

Dickie tapped his nose.

'You leave it to me. Just leave that to me.'

Like I was holding me breath. Dickie never did anything for me fer nothing and he wasn't going to start now.

I made Lily a jam sandwich and told her she could watch telly. I was hoping she wouldn't notice there wasn't much food for tea. Sometimes, when I only had a jam sandwich to offer, we played princess tea party 'cos she always chose jam then. I gave Dickie a cup of tea, more from habit then anything. I could hear him asking Lily about school while I was getting ready fer work. I never worried - not exactly, but I hoped Dickie wouldn't do anything to my daughter. Not like he had to Alfie. But she was still so little and he wouldn't be interested in her. Only the worst kind of pervert would have touched my Lily.

I was right Mummy...he couldn't get inside me because I wriggled and hit him and screamed and he couldn't...you know...do it. Alfie must have seen what was happening because he started to fight the man off me but I don't think he saw the knife. Then my stomach felt as if it had been sliced open. I think they both fell on me and the knife went in me. I remember I couldn't breathe 'cos they were both so heavy...It really, really hurt.

Lottie

I'd decided to change and put on something clean. I put a hot-brush through my hair so that the hairdresser wouldn't get a fright and dug out the summer sandals I'd bought in Madeira. I shaved my legs and painted my nails and thought the diary was going to be so full of improvement it might go up in smoke. It made me smile in spite of myself. I put on my eyes and some lipstick too.

I don't think I realised at the time, but that was a milestone moment. It was the first burst of energy I'd experienced since Saskia was admitted to hospital and it felt good. The eye-bags were paler than they had been but my skin was dry and uncared for and would take more than a quick fix. I was probably only getting about three hours sleep each night so no wonder I looked haggard. I felt like a piece of driftwood dumped by a scummy tide most days. But this was a good day wasn't it? I was up and about to 'pull myself together' as Dad would say. Poor Mum and Dad. It was especially hard for them. At least Tom and I could visit Saskia regularly, but for them it was a two hour journey from Cirencester when they could squeeze time out from the farm. Not easy with a herd of two hundred dairy cows. And when they got to us there was nothing they could do but sit and look at their only granddaughter as she slept.

It was a warm day and I was pleased I'd planted bulbs in the patio tubs. I noticed for the first time they were making quite a show. Tom had told me how lovely they looked and he was right. He constantly encouraged me to regain a semblance of my former self; the one who used to be the life and soul of any gathering. 'Why not try a walk today

Snooks? Inspect the fruits of your handiwork. Bring some flowers into the house.' I couldn't imagine having flowers in the house. It felt disloyal to Saskia...

I needed to visit my daughter earlier than usual that day so that I could visit the hairdresser and be back in time for the drinks party. Saskia was lying there, beautiful, peaceful as usual; she was my very own sleeping beauty. We were lucky to have the privacy of a side ward so no stranger was watching and no one stared at a girl who wouldn't wake up. I noticed a nurse had brushed her hair and the fragrance of soap told me she'd had her bed bath. As I took her fresh clothes from my backpack, I stared out of the hospital window. Her room was above the Accident and Emergency department where a constant stream of ambulances came and went. Over the weeks I'd become a voyeur, intruding on other peoples' misery.

I made sure the nursing staff knew I'd arrived and told them I was going to put clean clothes on my daughter. I'd learnt from the nurses how to dress and undress Saskia which involved a rolling technique while her clothes were taken-off and new ones added. It was simply one section at a time. I always preserved her dignity; everyone did. We treated her as if she was awake.

A lovely Thai nurse who always greeted us with a beaming smile, popped her head around the door. 'Good afternoon Ping, I don't suppose there's any change?' I asked her. I knew there couldn't be but I always asked.

'Nothing today Mrs Hanson. But we all hope for good news.'

Hmm...I negotiated all the tubes attached to Saskia and took her cardigan off by rolling her gently towards me and then away. I put it on the chair. She was in joggers and a blouse which were easy to dispose of as I took her in my arms and told her that today the sun was shining and I was having my hair done later. I changed her pants and eased her pink cotton dress away. When she was first admitted I'd asked the sewing department at school to open all her blouses, tee shirts and dresses on the side her tubes were attached and they put Velcro fastenings on to make the dressing process easy.

'Can you manage?' Staff Nurse appeared. 'Here. Let me help.'

Saskia looked so pretty in pink. I put her soft ballet pumps on her perfect feet and gazed at my daughter.

'There's always hope, you know.' Staff was trying to cheer me up and I smiled to reward her.

'I know. But hope runs a bit thin, sometimes.'

'I'll make you a cup of tea Mrs Hanson. Are you expecting your husband?'

'No. He won't make it today.'

She disappeared while I held Saskia's hand and fought the tears.

'I brought your perfume darling again. I'm going to make you so fragrant all the medical students will want to date you. I'll spray your hair too.'

I painted her nails and told her the news from home. I told her a funny story about the new boy Anderson who was trying to climb out of the dorm window when a prefect caught him and pulled the sash window down so hard that he wriggled like a little piglet. I was just about to tell her how lovely the garden was looking when there was a loud beep which scared me half to death. I called a nurse in the corridor and she quickly discovered the ripple mattress had stopped its constant wave of motion. She expertly un-plugged and then re-plugged it and the alarm stopped. My heart was racing and my mouth was dry; I thought Saskia was having a heart attack. But then I saw her body continue its gentle undulation which assured me all the mechanics were working again.

'I might as well turn her now I'm here.'

I stood aside while the nurse put my daughter onto her side.

'Wow she smells lovely. Sorry I smudged her nails,' she said, noticing my bottle of nail varnish.

'I'll sort it. It's no problem.'

'Nice colour. It matches her dress. Makes a change for her to wear a dress, doesn't it.'

'I thought so. She's a real girlie-girl and I'm fed up with her joggers and tops. I want her looking nice when...'

'Of course you do.'

'There'll be hell to pay if she wakes up and looks a mess.'

'I'll bet. If she's anything like my niece. Remember to keep talking to her Mrs Hanson. You never know... you might trigger something positive.'

I wondered if Saskia's adoption details were on her notes. Would anyone think it was relevant? Did people start pointing fingers at adoptive families when things went wrong? I had never considered there to be any essence of 'nature' in our daughter, only 'nurture', but common sense told me there had to be both. When Saskia's adoption was finalised, no birthmother access was requested so none was given and secretly, we were relieved. We knew her father was heavily into drugs but had no indication that her mother indulged.

The details of how, when and where we would tell our daughter she was adopted had been teased apart and reassembled until it was a sleek manuscript of love and responsibility. Every relevant book on Waterstone's shelves was digested to ensure we were sensitive and qualified adoptive parents; we didn't anticipate any hiccups. The social worker warned us that sometimes the big revelation doesn't go according to plan but we both thought that wasn't likely to happen in our family.

We decided Saskia would be told while having our summer holiday on Tresco in the year that she turned eight. Being on holiday was always the happiest and most relaxed time of the year so why not tell her while sifting powder white sand through our toes on a sunny day? If Saskia asked, and we doubted she would, we could truthfully tell her we had few details of her birthparents. But when the moment presented itself, we were walking on Bryher and struggling over the hilltop to Hell Bay for a picnic. Tom broke the news of her heritage using the words we'd rehearsed a thousand times and I was right, Saskia had very little to say. She took the revelation in her stride and visibly warmed to the sound of being 'chosen'. But soon, even that became boring and the subject was dropped.

As I drove to the hairdressers I had a stupid idea that now Saskia was in her pink dress, she'd wake up. Of course, I knew real life didn't include fairies and unicorns and that I would be disappointed; under the surface I was a realist, despite the weak, fluffy exterior I was displaying to the world. But it was an idea that nagged away like a painful tooth. Pink dress equalled Saskia waking up. Stupid. What I needed to do was get more organised and get my life back into some semblance of order. I needed to be strong and stable when Saskia woke. But then I remembered that could be months...years even.

Ally my hairdresser was delighted to see me.

'We all wonder how Saskia is Mrs Hanson. We miss seeing you both so much.'

I smiled. Of course I smiled when people were kind. 'Thank you Ally. There's no real change but we're all hopeful. I'm hoping you can work a miracle on me today, too.'

'No problem at all. Could do with a trim I think. Shall I take the ends off?' She feathered her expert fingers through my hair.

'It may need more than a trim. I don't mind if you get the garden shears to it!'

'Perhaps we'll not be that radical. Candice is ready to wash you now.'

I seated myself at the basin and allowed the nimble fingered apprentice to soothe me. I relaxed and enjoyed the shower of warm water amidst the fragrance of expensive shampoo.

'Plenty of conditioner please,' Ally called across the salon. 'Use the leave-in one Candice.'

Now I knew I was in desperate measures.

I exited from the salon not only with all the local gossip, but feeling a new woman. What is it about freshly styled hair that makes women feel so good? For a fleeting moment I believed life was normal.

Tom was home before me and was making himself a cup of tea in the kitchen.

'How was she Snooks?'

'No change but I put her pink frock on and she looks very glammed-up. I think she would live up to her own exacting standards today.'

Tom kissed me and stood back to admire my hair. What a dear he was to notice. 'Wow, you look great. Would you like a cuppa?'

'Please. I'm coming with you this evening,' I announced. He dropped a teaspoon and grinned as if I'd peeled my clothes off and draped myself across the kitchen table. His eyes actually lit-up.

'Well done. Well done darling. I think we may both be turning a corner.' He kissed me again and I could swear he was damp eyed. 'Got a bit of marking to do and then I'll be up for a shower.'

'We haven't got long.'

'I know. Half an hour, max. OK?'

Drinks weren't until six thirty which gave me time to armour myself for the onslaught of, 'How are you Lottie? Are you coping my dear?'

People meant well but Saskia's coma was virgin territory on most people's radar. I guessed Tom had had it tough trying to explain to the higher echelon of the college how his daughter was knifed and fell into a drug and alcohol fuelled coma. It must have been excruciating for him. Churchill's was rife with drug-awareness programmes and susceptible lads whose parents spent a fortune to educate them. I worried he could have lost his job.

I was dreading the half term parental onslaught. Tom had written to parents of boys in our house to explain what had happened to Saskia. I didn't see the letter although I suspected it was sparse on detail. And of course parents would be concerned, and rightly so. One or two had already been to see the Head to discuss the situation and I knew I'd be worried if the tables were turned and it was my son living in our house. I would definitely expect my child to be kept safe at Churchill's College and might even question the competency of a House Master whose daughter fell into such bad company.

Failure never sat well with Tom. He never discussed with me how colleagues accepted the news but then, we hadn't had many meaningful conversations at all. I had no idea how my oyster-shell husband was coping with his life and that alone piled further guilt on me. I hadn't been there for him for weeks and could only imagine he'd had embarrassing moments within the work place. Perhaps I should have asked more questions.

'Of course I can do this.' I stared at my reflection in the mirror and took a long hard look at a face etched with grief; it was a face that had aged ten years in a few short weeks. The hair looked good though. I'd promised myself that the drinks party would be a turning point and I was determined to grasp the moment and make solid strides towards getting my life back. Sadly, that wouldn't change the course of Saskia's coma, but it would make for a better atmosphere in the house and perhaps it would stop me drifting like a yacht with no rudder.

I wanted to find something stunning to wear to the drinks party to boost my confidence and also to please Tom. He'd found it hard to hide his irritation with my inability to get on with life, but I'd always found his slightly anal view of things endearing, especially when I studied his ghastly mother and realised he was a miracle of manhood, all things considered. Despite being born to wealth and position and his mother's domineering ways, he had grown into the man I loved. And I knew he loved me. He showed it in little ways although he wasn't given to grand gestures. But I knew he'd be devastated if our marriage fell apart, even though neither of us had the tools to keep it together at that point. My mother told me not to worry. She thought our marriage was built on strong foundations and would, without doubt, survive. I hung on every positive I could find.

Things weren't good in bed, but who could wonder at that? Sex had always been healthily frequent and modestly enthusiastic on both our parts. But post the Saskia trauma, our time in bed meant nothing more to either of us than attempting to sleep and the endless task of shutting out the nightmare that defined our precious daughter. There was no touching, no cuddles, nothing between us that vaguely resembles foreplay; just the occasional robust effort at penetration from Tom and a sort of acquiescence on my part. It never failed to amaze me how men can screw at the drop of a hat. They screw if they're angry, screw if they're on a high and screw if they need to forget. I couldn't be like that. A cuddle would have been a start. Just a touch that wasn't sexual could have got things moving along a bit, but to expect full blown sex was like asking me to climb Mount Kilimanjaro without first burning calories at the gym and toning my body for the onslaught.

It was obvious I'd scored brownie points by joining Tom for the drinks party as he showered me with the enthusiasm of a first date. I'd chosen white linen trousers and a turquoise cardigan over a grey vest with a delicate sprinkling of diamanté around the neckline. I added chunky, white beads, grey heels and a generous spray of L'eau de Issey. I knew my husband appreciated how I looked.

'Love the outfit. Your look great Snooks. Just great.'

Tom ushered me out of the house at two minutes past six thirty. He treated me like a princess, albeit a fragile one who needed pampering. His arm around my shoulder felt reassuring in my current, cockeyed world. I knew I'd lost weight for the first time in years and despite my reluctance to look in mirrors, I'd sneaked an admiring glance as we left. I noticed, with satisfaction, the slim line hips which made

the boobs look rather plumptious; it was an illusion for sure
- but rather nice.

Drinks with the dinosaur were not altogether unpleasant
despite my embarrassment about our wayward daughter.
Beaks and their wives were pussy-footing around us and
only the brave actually referred to Saskia. I'd never been
good with pitying looks and even less well disposed to
educated males trying to show their sensitive side. So I
gravitated towards Heidi Brooker who was always good for
a bit of schoolboy humour. She had a disarming way of
getting to the nub of things without offending.

'Great to see you out Honey.' She kissed me on both
cheeks. 'You look fab darling and so sexy.

'Do I remember the connotations of sexy?' I asked her.

'Yeh yeh. Come off it Lottie, you and Tom are the couple
most likely. You know, everyone thinks you have more than
your share.'

I chuckled.

'I thought of you this morning. Hope you weren't listening
to Radio 4.'

I hadn't been listening. I rarely bothered with TV or the
radio. 'No. What did I miss?'

'Nothing you'd have wanted to hear. That sixth former
from St. Katherine's in Oxford. The one who was missing?
Her body's been found in the river and her mother was
being interviewed'.

'Poor thing. I'm not sure public dissection helps, to be
honest.'

'Guess you always hope someone will throw a ray of light
on evil, though.'

'Mm. And of course they might.'

'Are you sleeping better?

'Much better. Hurray for Amitriptiline.' Why would I tell
anyone the truth about the nocturnal elf that hammered
me with his doom and gloom antics?

'How are things with Tom?'

Trickier this one. 'We're managing. You know.'

'Bet you can't wait for half term.'

'I can't, but I think teaching helps Tom. It starves him of time to ponder. Unlike me. I'm due a degree in pondering any time soon.'

Heidi smiled. 'Let's ponder another glass of bubbly shall we?' She helped herself to two glasses of champagne and wouldn't take no for an answer when I told her I'd had enough. 'After all you've been through? Get it down you Mrs Hanson!'

I noticed Tom was in deep conversation with the Head and another teacher whose name escaped me. Tom caught my eye and gave a brief wave. I knew he was keeping a close eye on me and who could blame him?

Heidi asked about Saskia and sympathised when I told her there had been no change. We talked about all the ramifications; nothing was off limits with Heidi. We talked about everything from Saskia waking the next day to having her life-support switched off. Good old Heidi. She'd verbalised my greatest fear and it was the first time the words had been formed. Everything else was in my head on the continuous loop system that had become deeply imbedded.

Suddenly Tom was by my side. He smiled at Heidi and Anne Tilsly who had joined us. 'Great to see her out, isn't it girls?'

They both agreed it was.

'I'm afraid I'm going to steal her away but coffee together could be on the agenda in the near future, couldn't it Snooks?'

I agreed it could. As I was walked across the grass, guided by Tom's strong arms, he whispered in my ear.

'Needn't stay long,' he giggled like a naughty schoolboy. 'Just showing up for one glass of bubbly is enough.' He smiled at me and winked. 'Or two or even three, if you like. It's high time you had a bit of fun, Darling.'

My low heels sank into the grass and I took Tom's arm for support.

'Don't think the Head will even notice if we slip away, especially as the randy old goat can't take his eyes of the new science teacher. He'll hardly notice who comes and who doesn't.'

The nibbles looked delicious although I wasn't persuaded to nibble. I quite liked my new hips. Vintage Crug in Waterford flutes were held aloft on silver trays by ladies of a certain age dressed in black with frilly white pinafores. Years ago, when Tom and I first arrived at Churchill's, my friends were amazed by their first brush with the establishment. 'God this place is stuck in the Middle ages!' was the cry. And probably it was. But I rarely needed to defend it in more recent years. I'd learnt to appreciate certain elements of life at Churchill's; the uniqueness, its provenance and the shear centuries of history melded into its stone-work still tended to impress all but the most jaded. I suppose I particularly approved of its ability to stay unmoved and solid in a world that was rocking on its axis. Recently, the solid aspects of the old place held a degree of comfort, a feeling of belonging.

We made our way to talk to Ed Fenton as I wanted to ask if the baby had arrived. I noticed a small girl running around her mother's skirts and remembered the scurry of excitement when we knew Saskia was definitely going to be ours. She was much the same age and certainly showed similar energy.

Preparation for Saskia's arrival reached manic proportions. We were lucky to have a large house and garden in which to welcome her and began by getting the maintenance staff to paint her nursery. Then they created a child-proof outdoors which had to be fit for a princess. Money flowed into Harrods and staggered out in the form of pink and white toddler paraphernalia delivered by polite men in vans. Nothing was too good for our new arrival.

'I expect the half term will be a blessing Lottie.'

I jumped as the deputy head smiled down on me with sympathetic eyes. At six foot six he tended to look down on most people, but he made me feel petite and vulnerable.

'I think so John. But to be honest, one day is much like another at the moment. The boys are definitely a distraction for Tom.'

'Any change? Any good news about Saskia?'

'Not yet but we're hopeful. Thanks for....'

Tom interrupted the conversation. 'I've just had a call from the house Darling. Sorry John, I have to deprive you of my lovely wife. We need to get back.'

'My loss Old Boy. Good to see you out and about again Lottie. Don't forget, everyone is here for you...you only have to ask. You've been missed.'

'Thanks John. You're very kind.'

Tom ushered me away and then started to giggle. 'That worked.'

'What? What worked?'

'There's been no phone call Snooks. I just it as an excuse to extract ourselves. Thought you'd be pleased.'

'I am.' I smiled at him. It was unusual for Tom to play hooky around school duties. I felt well rewarded for the effort I'd made.

We walked home and took the shortcut around the gym and across the tennis courts. I could see the river on its never-ending journey through the willow trees and realised it had been weeks since I'd walked that way. I decided to walk somewhere the next day, even if it was only to the shops.

The house was quiet, as it should have been when we arrived back; all the boys were doing their evening prep. I caught a look from Tom that told me he had one thing on his mind and, happily, I found I could cope. No, I could do better than cope; I was looking forward to it.

Tom found the junior master who'd been housesitting and told him we were home. The young, bespectacled man scurried off, no doubt to do a pile of marking or lesson preparation for tomorrow. I offered my services to ensure all was well with the boys.

'Shall I check on the sixth form common room for you?'

'Thanks. They always prefer it when you stick your head round the door. I'm not flavour of the month at the moment. Not since I vetoed the end of term party.'

'I'll do it then. I'll see if Lovett is back after tea with the grandparents, too.'

'You're an angel. Just check that Lamperton is around. He has a tendency to skip off to town on Thursdays. Some girl, I think, who waits by Marks and Spencer for him.'

'Spoil sport! I'll see if he's in. Shall I cook? Chef's left us a salad but I can probably do better than that.'

'Umm. That would be good.'

Tom always had a good appetite after sex. I raided the freezer for some fish and a chocolate sponge pudding that I intended to puddle in chocolate sauce. It would really make Tom's night.

My husband was full of high spirits. He locked our apartment door and put the 'see matron' sign up. I was a bit giggly having eaten very little all day and not bothered with alcohol for weeks. Champagne had gone straight to my head. And then, taking me by surprise, Tom scooped me up like a bride and plonked me playfully on our huge bed. Enid had changed the sheets that morning I noticed, which always enticed my husband.

I could see us both in the dressing-table mirror and a slight feel-good-factor lifted the burden on my heart. That was surely a step forward I told myself, even if we knew we had the champagne to thank for our enthusiasm.

Tom kissed me and I kissed him back. He stroked my cheek and lifted my hand to his lips. 'You're still as beautiful as the day I married you. I'm going to take better care of you.'

I wanted to make a smart remark about wrinkles and eye-bags but I bit it back and kissed him with such enthusiasm that we tumbled like kittens across the fresh linen. He slid the cardigan off my shoulders and kissed the nape of my neck. Tingles shot across my shoulders. His fingers eased one strap of my vest down my arm and I helped with the other. Soon he reached for my breast and took a nipple in his mouth. I felt the effect somewhere alien; there was a pulse that hadn't played a role in my life for weeks. Tom shed his own clothes like a teenager and left them in a pile on the floor. I constantly told the boys to refrain from doing that but this was my fully-grown, sexy husband and he wanted to fuck me. I was grateful. Grateful that he still wanted the miserable specimen I'd become and I was grateful that maybe, just maybe I could get a life back, regardless of what had happened to Saskia. He eased my trousers over my new, slim line hips and his fingers searched around the lace on my thong.

We both needed the bodily contact and what began as soft and delicate became urgent and thrusting and ended with an apology from Tom for the speed with which he climaxed. I smiled at him and told him it didn't matter. I thought it was a miracle it had happened at all and felt a glow of pleasure or maybe more a feeling of relief that we'd made it that far. And bloody Alfie Collins was nowhere in sight.

Tracey

I was so worried about my boy I decided to make a second visit to the prison the next day. I rung them and said it was urgent because I was worried and they agreed I could pick up a visiting order at Reception when I arrived.

The number fifteen bus was late so I nearly missed me connection and it was bloody bucketing down again. I 'spose I was lucky I got there in time. And there was one hell of a queue to get in and the dogs were sniffing about. As if I'd be daft enough to bring drugs in. They made a young girl with a baby take off the kid's nappy to check for something. I thought, OMG, surely they don't smuggle drugs in on their kids?

There were lockers we had to use when we got in. Everything had to go in them, including handbag and coats. It was so we couldn't pass anything across to prisoners. A woman was patting down the female visitors and I wished she'd hurry up. I couldn't wait to see my Alfie. Although he was tough and street wise, this was all new to him and he'd looked dreadful when I'd seen him the day before. I worried all night.

A bloke in a long overcoat was gobbing-off, 'How much longer have we got to wait?' When nobody answered he got beside himself and used some ripe language and ended up being marched off by the screws. I sympathised with him 'cos it was like the staff were on a go slow. I dug me ID from me bag ready for my turn at the check-in and waited. I just waited. The officer looked a miserable cow; it was the same one as the day before and I hadn't seen her smile once. You needed yer visiting order and a photo ID to get in and she looked like she hoped I'd forgotten mine. But the visiting order was there, waiting for me.

Annie Etheridge told me not to eyeball anybody then they can't pick a fight. I couldn't see anybody likely to do that. There was a posh old couple behind me and all they kept talking about was, 'when, Anthony was little'. Yeh well...all our sons were easy when they was little.

The sniffer dog took no notice of me, thank goodness as we passed through to the Visit's Hall. It was like being in a huge porta-cabin. A bit like an aircraft shed, I thought. And I could see my Alfie was sitting with a bright yellow waistcoat on, same as yesterday. I wanted to hug him but I knew better. Instead he gave me a wink like there was nothing to worry about.

'So how are things then? A simple enough question but it opened the floodgates. Everything about that place came tumbling out like he'd kept it bottled up until he could tell me.

'All I can 'ear is the clanging of keys; metal grating in locks.'

I noticed he was awful pale. It didn't help that they dressed them all in dishwater grey.

'It's just like on the tele in here and...to be honest Mum, I'm scared shitless.'

If my Alfie was scared then I knew it was bad.

'The trouble is,' he said, 'I don't know how long I'll be in here.' It made it hard for both of us to get our heads around things. The real worry was knowing he could get anything up to ten years. That was what his brief said.

'But I never fucking did it Mum. I love her.'

I looked at him and searched those deep brown eyes. It sounded like the truth to me, but it would to his mother, wouldn't it?

'I'm gonna plead not guilty. Corse I am. I never done it.'

It broke me heart to see him. He was angry. I could see it in his eyes and I could understand it, too.

'I saw you in court but you never smiled at me once.'

He sounded like a little boy

'I was too damn scared to smile. And I was hoping they'd grant you bail. I held my breath while we waited to know. Snotty cow of a judge, wasn't she? When she remanded you I was angry,' I told him. I looked at his little face and wanted to put my hand over his, but I dared not touch him. 'Little people like us never get a break, do we?'

'You had a look on yer face like you used to give me when I was a kid. When I lied and you sussed me? Remember? Well, you've got it wrong this time Mum 'cos I never done it.'

'I never thought....' I tried to spit the words out.... 'I was just wondering why your prints was on the knife.'

'Ha. Thought so. You think I did it. I knew it.

I could feel tears trying to have their way on me face and I looked out the window. 'Alfie,' I tried again, 'you need to know I'm right here fer you. No matter what happens. OK?'

He didn't answer me and I was desperate for him to know I'd got his back.

After a while he was ready to spill it again. It was like he was battery-charged. 'Thing is Mum, now they've found my fingerprints on the knife, no matter how many times I tell 'em what happened, nobody believes I tried to save Saskia. I grabbed the knife to stop that wanker hurting her.' I could see tears in his eyes. 'And next thing I know, she's bleeding like a stuck pig. My beautiful girl was bleeding in front of me eyes. I was so scared Mum. I had no idea what to do.'

I was imagining the scene. It must have been mayhem.

'She kept screaming at me to leave her alone. She screamed like a demented animal. I wanted to stay with her but she was making so much noise... I ran. I ran so fast my brain couldn't keep up with me. I wanted to find you 'cos I knew you'd know what to do.'

He was getting agitated just remembering it all.

'Keep it down over there.' A big bloke in uniform eyeballed us.

'Wanker.' Alfie flashed a look I'd seen a million times before. I was pleased he still had a bit of spark left in him.

'Why it never crossed my mind to dial 999 I'll never know. I never seem to latch on to doing the right thing in a crisis, do I? And 'cos I didn't do the right thing, Saskia might die. I'm stuck in here and I want to see her.'

I watched the officers as they scanned the room. They eyeballed us like we were all criminals. There was a woman doing teas and I wandered over to get a couple. They had to be free 'cos they'd taken everybody's handbag away.

'There's nothing to do in here,' Alfie said. He slurped his tea and made a face. 'Shit, ain't it? Why the hell can't they make a simple cup of tea? There's nothing to do in here Mum. It's driving me nuts.'

He started to tell me about life on the wing, like he needed to get things off his chest. He chuckled when he told me about a screw working her way along the landing that morning. He said you could hear her two cells down.

'Get out Osborne and wash your filthy self,' she yelled at the top of her voice.

'You can hear everything in here. And she's right. Osborne stinks. My door flew open like she wanted to take it off the hinges. 'Shower, Collins.' And then I heard myself say 'Yes Miss.' Can you imagine me saying that?'

I couldn't. Made me chuckle as I watched a dark cloud cross the window. Looked like it might rain again, soon.

He told me, 'I picked up my wash stuff and followed her along the landing like a little kid.'

He made me laugh despite the grimness of it all.

'You ain't never toed the line since you was a nipper so I don't think you'll be starting in here,' I reminded him. But he seemed determined to tell me the tale of going to the showers. I told him to keep his voice down a bit.

'Officer Pershore is butch and meaty,' he said. Blokes in here love her but she ain't nothing like any sexual fantasy I've ever had.

It felt too much information from my grown-up son but I was there for whatever he needed to get off his chest. I looked at the snooty cow on point duty to see if she'd heard him, but she was too busy talking to another screw to notice us.

I could sense Alfie wanted to tell me more. It was like he'd had nobody to talk to for days.

'According to Crunchy, it's only a matter of time before I start fancying her. They all want to give her one.'

I couldn't help smiling even if it was a bit near the mark. At least he'd cheered up a bit.

'Look at the tits,' Crunchy said. 'Forget the large ass and concentrate on the tits man.'

'Ssh! You'll get locked down if you keep on.'

I asked him what his cell was like. Was the bed comfy? Anything to change the subject.

'It's OK. I'm sharing with a miserable sod who tried to get the night safe out of Barclays Bank. Idiot.'

Then he told me how he had to give all his possessions the quick once over every time they took him out of his cell.

'The thieving bastards in here'll nick anything. And the screws spin your cell whenever they want. But I'm not daft. I've hidden me slicer somewhere they'll never find it. You have to get savvy pretty quick in here otherwise they find all yer illegals.'

'What slicer!'

'Ssh Mum, keep yer voice down.'

He looked around like a ferret to see if I'd attracted attention. He leaned over the table as far as he dared. 'You have to learn to look after yerself. It's bloody dangerous in here. And it cost too much to get hold of a slicer to let the screws find it.'

It all sounded like something off the tele to me, but the words were falling from his mouth like vomit. I wanted to ask what he planned to do with the slicer but the words got stuck in me throat. But there was no shutting Alfie up.

'You have to blag stuff off the blokes and that costs money. Or a splif, if you've got one. You can get most things done for a splif. Now I've got something to hide, I have to be bloody careful.'

I could hardly believe what I was hearing. I thought the silly sod was going to get caught doing something he shouldn't and then they'd eat him for breakfast. I knew he was heading for trouble.

'Now you listen to me,' I told him. 'Don't you think it's bad enough being in here, without making matters ten times worse? Keep yer bloody head down, you pillock.' I could feel me temper rising but I dared not make a fuss. 'I better go before I say something I'll regret. You'll keep your nose clean, if you know what's good for you.'

And I missed the bloody bus home.

The horrible man got off me and I didn't see him again...
Alfie wanted to take the knife out of my stomach and he

*tried to stop the bleeding with his shirt. I remember
screaming. I...I wanted you to come and find me but you
didn't... Alfie said I should go with him and he'd fix me up,
but I was so scared... I could feel how much blood was on
my dress and I was afraid I was going to die. I still felt
dizzy... probably because I'd drunk so much vodka.*

Lottie

Over those terrible weeks I had convinced myself I wasn't a
good mother. I constantly felt guilty for not knowing what
my daughter was up to. But it wasn't that we hadn't
considered Saskia's imminent adolescence and her pending
sexuality. Of course we'd prepared ourselves for our
responsibilities as she grew from the small girl into a
blossoming young woman. Well, we were as prepared as it
was possible to be.

There was constant debate about where Saskia should be
schooled when she was eleven. 'If she doesn't get away this
year', Tom said, 'we'll have raging hormones in the house
which will keep us awake at night. I can't cope with a
teenager creeping around dorms in the early hours of the
morning to fulfil lustful urges she's too damned young to be
feeling.' Prophetic, I called it many years later.

We both recognised the need to give our daughter a more
balanced view of life which inevitably meant an all-girl's
school. So at the age of eleven, and after much soul
searching, Saskia was sent to boarding school in
Cheltenham. Having her grandparents in nearby Cirencester
went some way to calming our anxieties. Now, we decided,
Saskia could have weekend exeats on the farm and enjoy a
rather more grown-up relationship with Granny and Pops. I
was keen for her to have some of the solid grounding my
parents had given me. I thought it would do my daughter
good to see how the other half lived.

The Way It Is

People often remarked that Tom and I proved the rule that opposites attract, and I suppose we did in many ways. We wove a path around all our differences and created a brand new tapestry filled with a life we both loved.

Tom and I met when we were undergraduates; both of us were gung-ho, 'take a bite out of life' students and we gelled like limpets on a rock. I never looked at anyone after I met Tom Hanson.

My husband had a silver spoon well and truly thrust into his delicious, sensuous mouth from the day he was born; Tom had free access to the world of gap-year travel long before it became the norm and he deferred his place at Oxford not once, but twice, (amazing what can be done when influence comes as standard down the family bloodline.) So he'd tipped up with more than an air of 'man about town'. Sports cars, suntans gained on the ski slopes and girls who hung on his every word were everyday fodder for a rather shy and unassuming Tom, and it was over a year before he noticed me.

I must say, money never spoilt him. He was a quiet, thoughtful man, especially wary of the giggly, blue-stocking-brigade. I remember he always looked put out by too much attention. Silly girls made him frown and excess in any form still makes him uncomfortable.

As the second son of titled parents he'd always known his elder brother would inherit both title and fortune. And he never cared. But their father died of cancer when Tom and his brother were both in their teens and his elder brother had to step up to the plate.

The responsibility of the estate barely touched Tom's life and offered him the gift of free choice. It was rather like an 'heir and a spare' scenario. He always thought he was the lucky one who was able to pursue a path that suited him, rather than being moulded into the Squire of the estate by an over-bearing mother. It was therefore an unbelievable shock when his brother died, shortly after we were married. When the reality sank in and the initial grieving was sated, we discovered his mother, or as I liked to call her, 'the grand dame,' had expectation that Tom would abandon his chosen career and return home to live on the estate.

Mother-in-law was already ensconced in the Dower House on the outer reaches of the estate but her proximity to our lives, if Tom did as she wished, left no margin for debate. Neither of us was prepared to risk our happiness. And so, much to his mother's amazement and barely concealed anger, Tom appointed a cousin to run the estate. We agreed that when the grand dame passed over we would reconsider our options but she was as strong as an ox and we would face that dilemma when it occurred. Meanwhile his mother bullied and harassed him to such a degree that we rarely visited her. I considered it to be her loss that she had never become close to Saskia, although I don't believe Saskia suffered by the decision.

While Tom was working through the more suitable girls at university and failing to notice me, I didn't let the grass grow under my size seven and a half feet. I was tall, gangly as a young giraffe and feisty with it. I worked hard but embraced student life to the full and I had a ball, literally, attending every party, function and college society going. Life at Oxford had limitations for me, mainly financial ones, but I managed to wring every last cent from my grant. When the money dried up there was always a willing suitor to step into the breach.

After life in parochial Cirencester, I couldn't believe the buzz of Oxford. As the daughter of third generation, working farmers, I had a firm handle on life without perks. Early morning milking for pocket money, helping with the harvest for the fun of it and calving a stillborn with the knowledge of a vet, all became second nature to me by the time I was thirteen.

'Don't know where the brains come from,' Dad frequently uttered. His pride in my achievement at the local grammar school knew no bounds and he slaved night and day to get the money required for me to live the life of an Oxford undergraduate.

'Just drop your mother a line now and then,' he asked. And I did. Religiously, every week I dropped a post card or letter into the box in the college wall and never failed to tell them what a great life they'd given me.

Mum and Dad became more precious, the older they got and I couldn't imagine a life without them. And for them, the violence bestowed upon Saskia was beyond comprehension. I managed to keep the details about the drugs from them at first, as I wanted to keep Saskia untarnished in their eyes. I knew they were desperate to be supportive but they just couldn't find a way. They were truly out of their depth.

Mum and Dad were thrilled when we chose Cheltenham for Saskia's senior education. 'I'll teach her to milk the cows on weekends,' Dad announced. 'You'll do no such thing,' Mum told him. 'She'll be a lady when she grows up. Tom has a title even though he don't use it. Remember that.' 'Twaddle,' said Dad and went to oversee the harvest.

Saskia threw herself into hard work in her new school; according to her letters and emails it was an endless round of hockey, lacrosse and tennis and an introduction to makeup, fashion and flirting. I didn't always show Tom what she wrote to me as he would have had words with her. If we'd had the large family we longed for, maybe he wouldn't have been so obsessive about our only daughter.

It took Saskia some time to catch up with her peer group's interest in boys. *What's so special about boys?* But eventually she began to view them in a more favourable light. We picked up the odd reference to a Dominic who'd taken her to the cinema and a Liam she met at a school social. All harmless, we were sure. Looking back, I know I was naïve.

About six months before she was due to make her A level choices, to everyone's surprise Churchill's decided to admit girls into the sixth form. This had been a major discussion point for years, especially by the died-in-the-wool crustaceans who never wanted change to their revered Churchill's College. But it gave us much to consider, not least the financial implications of moving Saskia back home. We would be entitled to considerably discounted school fees.

When we consulted Saskia about the new possibility, she told us she could see advantages in both schools and asked us to make the final choice for her. Eventually, it was agreed that she would take her A levels at Churchill's and we duly gave a term's notice to Saskia's school. We looked back on that decision later and realised we had made a mistake, but we could never have foreseen what a catastrophic decision it would turn out to be.

As she entered her first term of sixth form at Churchill's, it was noted that Saskia had blossomed into a confident young woman with no sign of the previous 'chummy' relationships with the boys in the house. Instead, she developed a competitive aloofness which calmed most of our fears. We told each other it looked highly unlikely Saskia would show any inclination towards the opposite sex for at least another year. How very wrong we were to bumble along our merry way, rejoicing in the fact that our darling daughter was home.

Saskia had always thrived in the masculine environment of Churchill's. When she was small she dominated the teenaged boys in the boarding house with her winsome smiles, tantrums and tears. But the lads loved her, often vying for the right to play football with her on the college lawns or to hold her aloft to cheer on the House in the annual boat race.

'I really should be jealous you know,' I frequently told Tom. 'She seems more content in the company of spotty adolescents than her own family.' Tom told me to think myself lucky to have fifty willing babysitters, all of whom would die to protect our daughter, should the need arise.

The Way It Is

At the age of four Saskia attended a local prep school just a mile down the road from where we lived. Money and privilege fluttered down on the pampered children like confetti. My Dad felt she should have gone to the local primary school, if only to keep her grounded, but we were more than happy with our choice.

Mum and Dad loved to visit but Dad was always like a cat on hot bricks around the boys. They had a tendency to call him 'Sir 'which was one step too far for a dairy farmer. Mum found it easier. 'They're just normal little boys underneath the plummy accent and the posh clothes', she often observed. And she was right. Over the years we'd sort a myriad of problems for the boys. Things that money and breeding had no armour against; heartache, divorce, deaths, abandonment and police cautions all came our way. But when some of the boys came back to see us as confident young men who had made their way in the world, we were as proud as any parent. They even brought their new wives and babies on occasion and I loved to see them all. Tom could be more aloof, but that's just Tom. I suppose Churchill's ways were more deeply ingrained in him than they were in me.

One morning I was drinking coffee when Tom appeared at the doorway 'Snooks. Ah, there you are?'

I glanced up from the kitchen table where I was looking up the family chocolate cake recipe.

'Hi. Didn't expect to see you. Everything all right?'

He looked at me for a full ten seconds; enough time for my stomach to flip and my mouth to dry-out.

'Oh God! What? What's happened?' I scraped the chair across the stone floor and went to him.

'Nothing. Nothing that I know of anyway. Mark Erdington wants to see us at eleven. I've got cover for my lessons.'

'Did it sound like bad news?'

'It didn't sound like anything Snooks. It was his secretary who called. Let's stay calm.

The transient joys of a few nights earlier seemed light years away and fear was stalking every cell in my body. But Tom played devil's advocate.

'You never know, it could be good news. Obviously, we'd have been called to the ward if Saskia had woken. But they could still have something positive to tell us.'

I didn't have a good feeling about it. I was racking my brains to remember if there were any test results due that day, but I couldn't think of anything.

'Have you had breakfast? You should eat something, Snooks.'

'You'd hate to stare at a puddle of vomit.'

'OK. You know best.'

Tom had made himself a bowl of porridge before school, as witnessed by the aftermath of milk and brown sugar, floating in congealed lumpiness in the sink. I'd always had an aversion to porridge.

'How about eating some dry toast? Something to line the old stomach eh?'

Darling Tom. Sometimes it was like living with my mother.

'I can't give food a passing thought. 'What if... they want to switch off her life support?' I blurted as warm, salty tears ran down my face.

'Hey. None of that. We're looking at the positives, remember?'

I didn't remember that conversation but I did remember every bloody thing I'd read about comas and I knew the day could arrive when there was no point in keeping the patient alive. That was fine for others, but not for Saskia. I'd fight with my bare hands if I had to, I'd do anything to keep my daughter alive.

'I'll have another coffee,' I said to appease Tom. 'Shall I make enough for you too?' He was deep in his own thoughts. It was easy to forget how tough it was for him as he always appeared so in control of his emotions. 'Would you like coffee? I repeated.'

'Good idea.' He smiled at me with his autumn-leaves eyes and slid his specs up his nose while he delved into the cupboard for a coffee mug. 'The traffic on the by-pass shouldn't be too bad at this time of day.'

I really didn't want the coffee but I gulped it down to please him. Coffee and breakfast seemed so mundane that morning. I asked myself, what if it was the day we had to say goodbye to her. Forever. It was more than I could bear and I headed for the bedroom to compose myself. Poor Tom, he hated to see me upset and he'd had rather a lot of upset to contend with over the past few weeks.

We set off in Tom's car because I don't think he trusted me to drive. I turned off the radio which was tuned to classic am as everything grated and annoyed. And then I thought about the radio; first it's on and then, at the flick of a switch, it's off, just like a life-support machine. It was as simple as that.

I tried to find something new to look at outside the car window on a journey we'd made a hundred times before. Make that a thousand, if you included trips to the hospital with boys from the House. I noticed a woman grab a small boy before he ran into the road. Hold on to him, I thought. Never take your eyes off him unless you want a tragedy in your family. I could feel hot tears forming in readiness to cascade down my blotchy face. I needed to get a hold on myself as I couldn't sit and blub in Mark Erdington's office. Tom would have been mortified. But actually, did I give a shit?

I spent the next five minutes remembering happier family times; the times before my daughter was at the mercy of medical people who could extinguish her life. A time before she invited that yob into her life. Whatever was she thinking? Not a question that would ever be answered, I suspected.

By the age of seven Saskia was, at best, precocious and often, downright demanding. I suppose we spoilt her as is the tendency of parents who wait for the gift of a child to come their way. And as she grew, so we and the boys loved her more. Saskia could spit venom as often as she'd grace you with her smile, but everyone forgave her the tantrums. By eleven she thought all boys were stupid and had a strong network of girlfriends; most had come up through the school years with her.

Saskia was always the tallest and the prettiest in her class. Well I thought so. Although her genes were not ours, she seemed to take after Tom with an innate slimness and height that promised to last, given a chance. My autumnal colouring was reflected in her face and she had my large feet. What were the chances of those similarities in an adopted child?

By the time we reached the hospital and found a parking space, my mind was made up. It was definitely going to be a life-support issue that was up for discussion and my adrenaline was pumping. As we made our way to the fourth floor it felt odd that we weren't visiting Saskia on the second. Mark's office was in the main corridor and his secretary was busy in the room next door to his. She smiled. 'Mr and Mrs Hanson? Mr Erdingham will only be five minutes. Can I get you coffee?' We declined her offer. Instead we sat in a hospital corridor observing the comings and goings of normal people. Those without a daughter lying in a coma. *I used to be like you*, I thought. *I had no worries. I had the perfect life.*

Mark appeared after a ten minute wait and we were seated in front of his desk with the door firmly closed. I'd never been good behind closed doors and my pulse thumped and sickness threatened. I gave myself a stern talking to and turned to Mark. 'This has given us both a scare. Being called in like this.'

'I know. I'm sorry Lottie. What I have to say has only come to light this morning.'

A sound escaped and I didn't know if it came from me or Tom. I felt his hand on mine and tried to gather comfort from the gentle squeeze.

'First I have to apologise.'

Shit, forget the apology and get on with it. Please.

'We missed something that should have been spotted earlier. There's no easy way to tell you but... Saskia is pregnant.'

I could hear a car alarm in the distance; it was probably in the hospital carpark and belonged to someone who just needed a simple x-ray. Probably, it belonged to a normal person, someone who hadn't had their world turned upside down for the second time in the last few weeks. I decided to wait until someone turned it off. I kept my eyes on the window although there was only a grey wall staring back. But it was firm and unmoving. It had no frills or complications. It was just a grey wall.

'Lottie.' It was Tom grabbing my attention and I appeared to have missed something.'

'Yes. Yes I heard. Saskia's pregnant.' The car alarm was still jarring on my thought process.

'Are you alright darling?'

I knew blood had drained from my face and I didn't trust my legs to function. There was no escape. 'Of course,' I said. 'What's another crisis? What else can life throw at us?'

I didn't feel it coming. Not one signal emerged to warn me before I curled my body onto my knees and sobs gushed from somewhere deep, low and painful. Tom wrapped his arms around me but they didn't make me feel safe. I thought I would never feel safe again. I was a pathetic human being and an abject failure as a mother. How much worse could things get? Did he rape her or did she lie on her back and open her legs to him? I tortured myself with hideous flashes of rampant teenage sex and fought the urge to vomit on Mark's floor. I noticed it wasn't carpeted so...that was all right then. A mop and bucket with some strong disinfectant would do the job. Still, no one had switched off that bloody car alarm.

I grasped the pristine white handkerchief Tom found in his pocket, curtesy of reliable Enid, and tried to mop myself up.

But the tears wouldn't stop. It was as if all the weeks of coping and putting on a brave face had crumbled into this moment.

'Tom, I'll give you a few minutes alone. I'm only next door.'

'Thanks. She'll be OK when I talk to her. I'll sort it out.'

'Of course.' Mark left us alone.

I suppose knowing that Tom would 'sort it out' should have been a crumb of comfort but it made me mad. I felt mad as hell with Tom, for no reason I could explain.

'Sort it out!' My voice was louder than he liked. 'This isn't one of your boys who's failed an A level. How can you 'sort it out? You're not bloody Merlin.'

'Lottie please. Not in here. We need to go home and talk about this.'

'It feels a bit late for talking. Don't you think?'

'I'll go next door and tell Mark we're going home. I think we'll need to see him again in a couple of days.'

'OK'. I'm still crying although the deep sobs have subsided.'

'That's the ticket Snooks. Why don't you pop into the ladies while I see Mark?'

'Um...I'll see you along the corridor then.'

I headed to the loo, more to look in the mirror than anything else but then I wished I hadn't bothered. I probably wouldn't bump into anyone I knew, so who cared that I looked like a demented hamster?

Tracey

Old Dickie's came to see if I was alright. Corse I wasn't alright. Me lad was inside.

'He says he don't want to see ya,' I told him with a smirk, after he'd settled his ass on me sofa. 'So don't you go near him.'

'I know,' he said. 'Some tart at the prison refused me a visiting order when I rang.' Said Alfie don't want to see me.'

'Why would he? Want to see you?'

'I wouldn't mind, but he's not got none of the things he'll need'.

'Like what? I can take them in.'

'Shan't fuckin bother. Got money has he?'

'Too much money. That's half his problem. Too much bloody money,' I told him.

'Well he shouldn't get in trouble then. Not if he's got money.'

'What sort of trouble?' I searched Dickie's eyes for signs that he was lying. I had plenty of experience of that.

'Don't know as I should tell you really. I only know 'cos me neighbour's nephew, Greggo Hewitt, is on the same wing.'

'And?'

'You sure you want to know? Don't whinge to me if you don't like it.'

'Corse I want to know. What'd you take me for? A wuss?'

'OK. Well...' Dickie took time to blow his nose. Snuffled and snorted like a hedgehog after milk. 'There's a nonce on the wing what's taken a fancy to your Alfie. Big bugger. Says he's got a passion for black haired youngsters. Likes your Alfie's skin, he said.'

'What! You gotta be kidding me. Alfie ain't no nonce.'

'Never said he was. This bloke takes what he fancies. They call him the 'shower- shagger' 'cos he catches the young 'uns when they're in the shower block.

I had to sit down. Alfie was a lot of things but he wouldn't go near a nonce. He'd had more women than I'd had hot dinners.

'Then of course, there's the drug gangs. Got any drug debt, your Alfie?

How the hell did I know?

'I can help fix it, you know.' I recognised that whining voice. And his eyes told me there was a catch.

'Oh yeh. And how can *you* keep my Alfie safe in there? Going in for a stretch, are yer?'

'Not me. But Greggo Hewitt's already in there, like I told you, and he's prepared to make a little deal with you.'

'Why me? What's he want with me?' Shit. I could feel things were taking a turn for the worse.

'There's lots of help you can get for the boy. Especially if you're prepared to do a favour in return. See what I mean?' he wheedled.

I kinda did but I didn't like the sound of it. Dickie went to put the kettle on, just like the old days. Thought he still owned me but a lot had happened since those days. I was older, stronger and could I cope with Dickie and his dirty little ways.

'There you go me little Pidgeon Pie.' He put two mugs of tea on the table. 'Seen yer mother lately?'

Now I was really worried. Dickie never asked after me mother. He had a sort of soft look about him, too. Well I wasn't going near his 'old man' - that much was certain. Those days were gone. Thought it would have shrivelled up to nothing, anyway.

'Sugar, Pidgeon?'

I never took sugar. I grabbed the mug and clasped me fingers round it. It was too hot to drink but I didn't want him shovelling sugar in.

'Spit it out then. Might as well cut to the chase.'

'Not so hasty. You always were hasty. Sometimes you've gotta just mull things over a bit. See how it fits.'

'So how exactly does it *fit*?'

'I'm just thinking how this could work. Best fer everybody. You know?'

I hadn't got a clue what he was talking about. 'Best fer you, you mean?'

'I could be hurt by that remark if I didn't know you. Luckily, I know yer don't mean it. Always spouting yer mouth off, ain't you?'

I couldn't argue with that. Mum always says I'd got a mouth like a barn door. She could talk.

'I still don't get it. Talk clear, will you?'

Dickie took a slurp of tea. I was sick to me stomach worrying about what was coming. He added another spoonful of sugar to his mug and made me wait.

'OK. ....OK.......It's like this. Greggo said he's got a little business what's going to waste. Needs a bit of help on the outside, you know?'

I didn't know, but I had a pretty good idea it would involve sex.

'He said he'll keep an eye on Alfie for you, he'll see no nonce gets him up the....well you know what I mean. Get me drift? But it depends if you can do a bit of business for him.

OMG. I could already imagine Alfie being hurt. He'd put up a fight for sure, but they'd love that, wouldn't they? Nonces. 'What sort of business?' I already knew I was done for. How could I let Alfie get hurt in prison?'

'Well here's the thing. Ever heard of SPICE?'

I shook me head. I wasn't letting on to him. Dickie chuckled.

This is...' He took time to blow his nose like a bleeding fanfare. 'Made in back room kitchens it is. You know it's real strong stuff? It's the best currency there is in jail at the moment. Prisons are rife with it, right across the country.

'I aint peddling drugs. I've got my Lily to think about. Who'd look after her if I was inside? Me bleeding mother? I don't think so.'

'No...... yer not getting it.'

'That's 'cos you ain't telling it straight, Dickie.

'OK. This is the thing. SPICE is passing round in prison like a whore's panties.' He's looking at me like I'm daft. Like I don't know nothing about drugs.

'Yeh. And?

'But it's got to be paid for, of course. Know how they do that?

I hadn't got a clue but had an idea I soon would.

'They take the money off the little woman indoors. Her left at home with the kids. That's how.'

In about half an hour, after two cups of tea and much wheedling by Dickie, I had the lot. The men buy the SPICE that's been smuggled into prison and the wives pay their bills. The deal on the table was that I set up a credit round, collecting money each week from the families of the prisoners. Sometimes I'd have to travel quite a few miles and they'd give me a car with me own driver. Dickie said they liked to have a woman call for the money 'cos it didn't look as suspicious as a bloke. The old bastard even suggested I take Lily with me. Like hell I would. He reckoned the Old Bill got wise to the game after a time, so I'd have to go careful. Not calling on the same day at the same time was important, he said.

I said I'd think about it.

'Don't think too long 'cos you never know who might be stretching Alfie a bit.'

Shit. Did he mean what I thought he meant?

I'd made Alfie leave me and then there was no one. I realised I should have gone with him. Then I started to feel really cold and sleepy and I didn't care anymore. I wanted to float away.....It felt as if I was in a huge balloon floating in the clouds. ...I...

Lottie

I knew the first real fall-out in our marriage was on the horizon. After our meeting with Mark Erdington and the devastating blow that Saskia was pregnant, the journey home was no more than a blur. But somehow we arrived at the house and Tom went to have a quiet word with Enid. I think he told her our news and suggested she went home

The Way It Is

early. I never agreed with his habit of treating her as a member of the family; I would much rather no one knew until we'd had time to discuss it, but that was typical Tom.

I inhabited a space in my own kitchen but it could just as well have been on the moon. It was the same kitchen where Tom had made coffee that morning and I sat in my usual chair. The scrubbed wooden table had familiar veins, lines and ink splodges that marked decades of other people's family crisis', but today it would need a knife to inflict a gouge deep enough to mark our family's distress. It had to be the worst drama that had ever been played out around that table. No. That wasn't right. If Saskia died, that would be the worst thing imaginable, but to allow those thoughts into my head was folly. It was more than my wrung-out body could cope with.

The view of the garden was unchanged. How was that possible? It was so calm and beautiful out there but it made me want to scream; I wanted to pull up the bulbs and slash the rose bushes to the ground. I wanted to be Saskia and disappear into a deep sleep. I'd rather have been anyone but me at that moment.

Tom was holding a bottle of gin. He didn't ask but poured two large ones. Even in our merciless state of despair, he managed to find ice and lemon. God forbid anyone in Churchill's drank gin without ice and lemon. He sat opposite me and watched as I gulped the top third of the content from my glass, all in one desperate slurp. It felt as if Tom was willing me to say something, but I couldn't.

'A termination is the only route Snooks. The sooner the better.' His look was one I'd learned to read over the years; a small frown rippled across his forehead, followed by a purse of his lips which made them momentarily lopsided. He hated it when I told him his mother had the same facial expression when she felt obliged to air-kiss me. No wonder our visits to the family pile were a rare occurrence. The worst thing was, I knew I was unlikely to win any argument when he conjured that look.

Would he take my silence as agreement? I stared out of the window some more. I visualised a sperm, valiantly swimming against the tide. It was a sort of *Finding Dory* moment; a small life on a mission of survival. I chose to ignore any ownership of the sperm or indeed the egg it was about to fertilise. And I didn't even equate it with my beautiful daughter. But I remembered how we longed for it to happen for us; we ached for a sperm to find the right egg, just one little egg didn't seem so much to ask, to have the child we longed for. But it never happened. How cruel Mother Nature can be and she'd certainly got a sense of humour. I couldn't answer Tom because I was numb. I knew exactly what he'd said but I was frozen by the thought that our grandchild could be scraped down a sluice.

'Snooks?' Tom puts his hand across the table and brushed my arm. 'You must know I'm right. What other option is there?'

I could see a new life in my arms; a bundle in white cloth that deserved the chance to live. What if Saskia's birth-mother had scraped away? We would never have had the delight of being her parent. And I wondered about our daughter. What was best for her? What would she want when she woke? I decided this conversation could wait for another day so made an excuse and left my husband sitting in contemplation at the kitchen table.

I couldn't ignore the irony of it all. We'd offered Saskia a new bedroom to welcome her home from Cheltenham.

'Why not take over the yellow guest room?' Tom suggested during her last term at Cheltenham. 'An en-suite and enough space for a sofa and a desk should make it feel rather grown up, don't you think?'

Our beautiful daughter bubbled with excitement at the thought of her new room. The next few weeks saw a flurry of college painters challenged to find the perfect shade of lilac to satisfy an exacting sixteen year old. She chose the same colour for the walls as the delphiniums near the rose trellis. I remembered the wind had got them that year. New furniture appeared, a four poster bed complete with drapes in the sheerest muslin and a pink carpet which I assured her would show every mark, but it was approved anyhow.

Saskia planned to access medical school after a gap year spent in some warm and exotic location, far from parental guidance, so her main A level subjects were the Sciences. It was therefore, just by chance, that she visited the college art-rooms with her father one Saturday afternoon.

'Give your old father a treat. Come with me to see the Art Exhibition in the Punchard Rooms,' he teased her.

'Sure. Could you wait while I change?' Saskia bounded off like a Labrador puppy to beautify herself. How she looked had become of vital importance to her.

'You come too Snooks. You haven't seen any of the boy's art this year.'

'I've promised to visit Belle. The new granddaughter is staying for the weekend and admiration is obligatory. Maybe next weekend.'

Tom waited for our daughter to appear in whatever dress was considered de-rigour to visit an art gallery.

'I must say, it's a treat to have half an hour or so of my daughter's undivided attention,' Tom said.

'Daddy! I'm always around these days.'

'Hmm.......It seems I always have to share you these days. I suppose when you have a beautiful daughter, everyone wants a piece of Saskia, don't they?'

'Daddy!' Saskia blushed.

I watched them saunter through the school grounds; they left me awash with a warm cuddly feeling which reflected our life since Saskia came along. Fourteen years of happiness was an unmeasurable joy. As father and daughter walked arm in arm, I remember thinking how lovely it was to see them so close.

As I changed for my coffee stop at Belle's, I imagined them entering the sanctified portal of student art, breathing in pungent turpentine, canvas, oils and paints. On every visit the walls quaked with Avant Gard ideas and Left Bank exotica. It was a world apart from the science labs where Saskia spent her working days.

If only Alfie Collings hadn't been painting next to the massive Gothic window, life could have been so different. Tom told me, much later, with unusually emotive language how the summer sun dappled Alfie Collin's face and rinsed an exotic shine through his raven curls. 'Cherubic,' he described him. He also noticed deep riveted lines across his forehead, which he thought were rather too many for one so young, but, he said they highlighted his concentration. I could only imagine the things he didn't describe such as a peep of pink tongue accentuating absorption in his work, broad shoulders and long, artist's fingers which were destined to touch my daughter.

Apparently, it was some time before Alfie acknowledged their presence. Only when he changed the colour on his brush did he raise chocolate eyes in their direction. Did just a beat of interest register? Collar length hair definitely set him apart from college pupil as did the tattoo of a serpent winding around his muscular left arm. He could never be mistaken for a member of the establishment.

Tom introduced himself and Saskia as they admired Alfie's massive canvass. Tom told me that, looking back, it was clear the crimson and black acrylic paint was of less interest to Saskia than the testosterone-fuelled young man. Isn't hind-sight a wonderful thing?

'You're.....um.....our special prodigy,' started Tom, at a loss to name the boy. Tom was hopeless with names.

'Alfie', he enlightened him without eye contact.

'Ah yes, of course. Alfie. I'm Mr. Hanson and this is my daughter Saskia'.

'Dad has a terrible memory for names,' Saskia laughingly assured him. Clearly her father had embarrassed her.

'I hear you're making quite a name for yourself around here,' Tom offered.

Apparently, Alfie didn't grace Tom with a reply but remained focused on his work. But he must have noticed

Saskia. How could he not? She was fresh as a daisy in a light, flowery dress which slipped over her curves like silk under her denim jacket. Her copper hair probably caught the same shaft of sunlight that lit Alfie's masterpiece, competing for attention and winning hands down. He couldn't fail to catch her fragrance which would have overshadowed the smell of oils, clay and adolescent boy. But now, it's all water under a bloody crumbling bridge. How could we have been so stupid?

A few days after the devastating news of the pregnancy, I realised I had to re-engage in a difficult conversation with Tom, no matter how painful it was. I couldn't waiver any longer; I had to say that one little word. The same one we hadn't said often enough to Saskia. 'No Tom, this baby will not be murdered in order to meet the exacting standards of Churchill's College.' Hmm... no wonder I had a problem finding the right moment, but this was one time I had to muster courage and do it.

The issue never deserted my brain, day or night. I knew I could deal with the scandal around college, although Tom probably wouldn't find it so easy. I had no idea, as he never talked about it. If someone in the establishment had challenged me about our daughter's behaviour I'd have said 'fuck it' and been happy to move on. We always had options, even if the mother-in-law from hell was one of them. However, the one thing I was certain about was my already-violated daughter would not be scraped clean of a living, breathing baby. Not while I had breath in my body. I thought maybe Mum and Dad would welcome her for the duration of her pregnancy but that felt a retrograde step. It was half a century ago since hiding pregnant girls in the countryside was common. I could see no easy solution, particularly as we were making decisions for a sixteen year old girl in a coma who had no idea she was pregnant.

The chemistry between Saskia and Alfie must have been rampant. I wasn't too old to remember first love and all its ramifications; the raging hormones and sleepless nights.

Teddy Arnold! The dude of the whole year, who never looked my way once. But if he had, would I have given him my virginity? Hmm...I'd been over and over that chance meeting between Saskia and Alfie Collings and sometimes thought I'd spotted a flicker of something different in her eyes when they came home that day. But my imagination was running riot. Neither Tom nor I knew that she slipped back to the art room and presumably, that was the start of their...their relationship.

It couldn't have been more than a week after that chance meeting that she persuaded Tom to buy a piece of Alfie's work. 'Five hundred pounds is a snip', she told us. 'One should always buy art from up-and-coming artists'. And still we didn't twig what was going on. Was life too busy for us to notice or did we have a rose tinted view of our daughter? Had we excluded the possibility that a boy like him could interest her? Whatever was going on in our heads I don't know, but we bought a piece of his art and had it hung in Saskia's bedroom. It was that money he later used to pay for his party.

Over the following weeks of misery I did nothing but doubt myself. And began to doubt the way Tom and I had brought up our daughter. I asked myself the awkward questions, the ones no parent ever wants to hear the answer to. Did we ever say 'no' to Saskia about anything? Was she so spoilt that she didn't know the meaning of the word? I remember thinking at the time that the livid colours of Alfie's canvas clashed horribly with Saskia's girly bedroom, but she didn't agree. Of course she didn't. Tom waffled-on that she was only stamping her personality on her room, when actually she was probably already screwing him. No wonder we were racked with guilt.

But that crucial conversation could be put off no longer. Tom spoke to Mark Erdington to say we needed more time before we met to make decisions, and the baby issue was eating us both alive. Whatever happened to 'talking things over' or 'knowing what the other was thinking? It seemed to have darted like quicksilver from our marriage. I suppose it was a blessing the boys had gone home for the summer. At least we weren't busy with school things. It was always bitter-sweet when they left for home, but this time it couldn't come too soon. Tom still had plenty to occupy him but it was easier to attract his attention during holiday time.

I booked a table in a restaurant renowned for passable food and asked for the 'snug table' which had a degree of privacy. I decided that was the time and place to tell Tom how I felt about Saskia's baby. Even saying those words made my stomach churn but hopefully, being in a public place would keep things calm.

'We don't usually book here Snooks. Fancy a change, did you?'

'Well, I thought lunch out might be nice. It feels as if we're exhaling now that term's ended. You look tired, but I shouldn't even mention it I suppose; I looked in the mirror this morning and I know what a sight I look, too.'

'You look lovely as always Snooks. Let's order shall we?'

I decided to wait until the main course was served before I broached the subject. I reckoned a good mouthful of food would be sufficient to staunch any outpouring of anger, on either part. Even though I wasn't hungry, I ordered a steak which would concentrate my mind on chewing. Tom's filet of John Dory looked delicious but required considerably less attention than the content of my plate.

'It's time to let Mark Erdington know about the abortion Snooks. The sooner the better don't you think?'

'No!' It had gone from my mouth like a rifle shot and it was too late to redact it. 'What I mean is... we haven't made a decision yet and anyway...I don't think she should... have a termination.' At least I got the words out but I didn't look at Tom's face.

There was the kind of silence I'd become accustomed to dealing with in my counselling sessions; the sort that occurred when a curved ball was thrown to put one off balance. But Saskia's baby was so much more than a curved ball.

'How can you even consider keeping this child?'

You'd have thought I'd suggested adopting a herd of delinquents.

'It's out of the question Lottie. You must know that.'

Tom was holding his knife and fork mid-air which was very non-you at Churchill's. I was determined to stand my ground.

'But I have a view too and I can't see this small life murdered because it's an inconvenience. Saskia was an inconvenience once. Have you thought of that?' I knew it was a low blow but it was about to get dirtier.

'This isn't an inconvenience Lottie. *This* is about to ruin our daughter's life. We have to act in her best interests.'

'And you know what that is, do you?'

'Of course I do. I'm her father.'

'And as her mother, I'm telling you we have to consider waiting until she wakes and then she can decide for herself. I'm not sure she'd want to scrape this baby into oblivion. Not sure at all.'

'Of course she would. She's not stupid Lottie. She'd see the folly of it all. What about her medical career?'

'She was born an unwanted child who was given the chance to live. Don't you think that will influence her decision?'

Tom pushed his John Dory to one side. 'Hell's teeth Lottie! Listen to yourself. You're suggesting our daughter, who's made this one mistake, must carry the consequences for the rest of her life? This child won't ever go away if we allow her to have it. She'll be an unmarried mother with all the ramifications that entails. I have no idea where your head is these days.'

Ouch! Well, I thought, let's try this for size? I opened my mouth and the words tumble like a waterfall. 'Let Saskia have the baby and we can care for it while she goes to med school. Does that sound so bad?'

'God Lottie. Is that what this is all about? Our inability to have a child is impacting on our daughter. How can that be right?'

My steak went the same way as his John Dory. So much for calm. I sensed that if I wasn't careful, this would become a full-on slanging match and Tom wasn't into such behaviour, especially in public. He summoned the waitress and asked for the bill. No pudding then.

Uncharacteristically he didn't hold the door for me as we exited which indicated the height of his anger. I was more than capable of dealing with a door and I stomped behind him to the car. As usual, I was thinking about Saskia. How the knife in her abdomen didn't harm the foetus I had no idea, but it was probably a sign that the baby was a fighter. It was a shrimp of matter with a fighting spirit and I was damned if I'd let it down. We travelled home in silence.

Tom scraped a chair from under the kitchen table and told me to sit on it. I did my Steptford wife impression and stared out of the window where I noticed the wind had got the roses. I should have tied them back. I noticed one in the corner by the fountain was the same pink as Saskia's favourite dress, but not as beautiful.

'Lottie, this nonsense has to stop.'

I was surprised he didn't bang his fist on the table. As I looked at Tom I wondered what the hell had happened to us. What was going wrong with our marriage? Bloody Alfie Collings was what.

There was a flush on Tom's face and his eyes were fiery. I knew he meant business, but so did I.

'What appears to be nonsense to you could be of monumental importance to Saskia. Have you thought of that? Can you live with being called a murderer when she wakes up and finds out what you've done?'

'There's no way she'll want to be saddled with a child. You know that.'

'Actually I don't.' I was icy cold and focused. It was as if my life depended on the next few minutes. 'I can't know for sure any more than you can what she'd want; this is life-changing stuff Tom and I vote she's given the chance to make the choice. She may wake up next week to find we've had her womb scraped because it didn't suit us to nurture her baby.'

'And she may not.'

Below the belt, that was one nil to my husband. I struggled because nothing I said was sinking into his academic brain. I tried again. 'OK. Let's look at the worst scenario. Say she never wakes but I.' Tears dripped down my cheeks but I pushed on regardless. An unattractive sniff escaped but hey, who cared? 'Let's say they want to switch off her life support machine. Well they won't do that if she's carrying a baby will they. It could buy her some time.'

'What part of *ethical* does that argument fall into?'

'What part of family loyalty, loving and caring and....' I stifled a sob, 'does your view fall into?'

'Lottie this has gone far enough.'

'No. Actually it hasn't. Think about this. If she never comes out of her coma, if we never have our daughter back, at least we will have her child. Her life won't have been in vain. Can you live with your decision if the worst happens?'

Tom left me sitting at the kitchen table mopping up a mixture of tears and mucous. I heard his car engine and wondered where the hell he was going. He shouldn't have been driving in a temper but I couldn't stop him. Actually, I wanted him as far away from me as he could get.

I decided to go and see Saskia. I needed to tell her what was happening in case she could hear me. I imagined a squeeze from her hand. 'Squeeze once for yes,' I'd tell her, 'and twice for no, darling.' Hmm... like that was going to happen. I made a cup of tea to calm me down before I drove to the hospital. All the mugs were in the dishwasher so I emptied it while the kettle boiled. The phone rang but I ignored it.

Parking at the hospital was the usual nightmare and I wasn't sure if I had enough small change so I asked a kindly gent if he could change a five pound note. He was happy to oblige. It still meant putting a pound too much in the machine and of course, it never gave any bloody change. It must have owed us fifty pounds at least.

I took a couple of deep breaths after parking and made my way to Saskia's ward. Sister was on duty and she smiled, 'Both of you today. Lucky Saskia.'

I gave her what I hoped was a smile but it could have been more a grimace as I realised where Tom had disappeared to in his fury. I should have guessed. Oh well, I knew he wouldn't shout at me in front of Saskia so I left the tin helmet at the door.

'Hi.' I spoke to Tom but my eyes were on our daughter.

'Hi Snooks. Come and sit down.' There was tenderness in his voice.

I walked to the other side of Saskia and held her hand and kissed her cheek. What I'd have given to see her green eyes sparkle with life. 'I need to change her underwear. Could you give us a minute?' I still hadn't looked at Tom. I dared not weaken.

'Of course. I'll get a cup of tea, shall I?'

'Thanks.' I pulled the curtains around her bed and busied myself. I noticed her hair needed brushing and I cleaned her mouth. When I'd finished I sprayed her with perfume and wondered if that was what bloody Alfie Collings found so irresistible. As Tom returned I swished the curtains against the wall and honoured my husband with a bleak smile. The tea was hot but that's all it had to recommend it.

'I've told her,' I lied. 'And she wants to keep it.' I engross myself in the plastic cup of tea. I knew I was playing dirty but there appeared to be no other way?

'I've just had a word with Sister. I mentioned we can't agree on the way forward and she suggests we involve Social Services. She said Saskia could be made a ward of court in the worst case scenario. Can you bloody believe that?'

I couldn't but I grasped the news to my advantage. 'I think that might be a good idea.'

'Why would we want them involved for God's sake?'

I smiled despite my misery. Just the thought of Social Services calling at Churchill's College amused me. It had undoubtedly never been known and was beyond poor Tom's comprehension.

'I've been doing some research,' I threw into the arena. 'We have to consider the rights of the unborn child. Did you know?'

'You're making this up Snooks. A bit low, don't you think?'

'How could you think I'd do that? The case is called the Frazer/Gillick competency. It's all on the net. Saskia's not the first under age girl in a coma to be pregnant.' My voice was rising until I remembered where we were. I whispered, 'it's true. I can give you the details if you want to read it for yourself.'

There was silence but I dealt with it. Great expense had been ploughed into my ability to deal with silence.

'No one else will make the bloody decision. That I can assure you.' Tom sounded as if he was addressing a class of boys.

'No one else as in *you*? Am I even on your radar?'

'No one else as in *us* Snooks. You know what I meant.'

And of course I did. But I'd learned years ago that when you can't compete on even terms with an academic, then you use instinct and emotion to find your way through the mire.

I kissed my daughter and went home.

Mummy, do you think I've got bad blood? Being adopted...you know. Is it possible I was born with drugs inside me? What if my...the woman who gave birth to me was addicted? Do you know anything about my birth parents? It's just that...when I was with Alfie it felt like... being ...home...where I belonged, somehow. I know it sounds silly...

I had to play a dirty game to stop the massacre of a tiny life as I knew Tom would play the long game to get his way. It terrified me that I'd be unable to stop him. Of course, I recognised my personal experience of longing for a child was informing my stance. No surprises there. But I knew it was more than that. With therapy came awareness and I'd suddenly recognised that during our marriage I'd capitulated over every major family decision. And I knew that my acquiescence had sometimes been detrimental to happiness. I'd lost the feisty personality I brought to our relationship, something I'd put it down to growing up and becoming a more responsible adult. Didn't everyone change after a few years of marriage? Had we become what Mum would call a 'marriage melded into comfortable togetherness?' Hmm... now that I was reflecting rather more than I used to, I was beginning to see a bullish side to my husband which wasn't attractive. Maybe the question I needed to ask myself was why had it taken such a monumental drama before I recognised it?

My life appeared to hold more questions than answers. Maybe I was picking at Tom because he was nearest to my anger. I needed to grasp reality before something else precious to me was damaged. But I was determined to hold firm on Saskia's baby. If she woke and didn't want to keep the baby, then she would have options; if we washed it down the plughole while she slept, she'd have no options at all. Of course, I hadn't yet asked myself if I could love Alfie Collins baby. That was one step too far at that moment. And if the baby was born before Saskia woke, would I be ready for that?

I rang Social Services and then I lied to Tom. I told him they contacted us and wanted to discuss the baby. But when the woman from social services came to the house, I made sure it was only me who kept the appointment. Talking Tom out of being there was easy. Social Services were anathema to him, not dissimilar to baby-snatchers or paedophiles. I still didn't believe he was acting in Saskia's best interest and I was convinced his first loyalty was to Churchill's reputation.

I wanted to hate Miss Social Services, otherwise known as Maddie Frost, but it wasn't easy. She arrived with a smile and a briefcase and was young, pretty and polite. The most important thing was, after only five minutes in her company I was convinced she had Saskia's interest at heart.

'It's not unusual for parents to disagree when a young girl gets pregnant. Often, they want different things but, of course, we have to make an informed decision about what your daughter would chose, if she was able. This case is an unusual one as Saskia can't convey her own view. It's so sad Lottie. I'll do everything I can to help.'

I believed she would.

Tracey

Old Dickie rang the governor and said he needed to see Alfie 'cos *'his mother was worried about him.'* He was such a conniving bastard and convincing liar that they bought his story and gave him a visiting pass.

Old Dickie was sitting at a table, ogling McCarthy's missus when Alfie was let in the Visiting Hall.

'How's it hanging Old Man? Tired of shagging me mother yet?'

'Pity your mother didn't teach you some manners.'

'She did, but I save 'em for people that matter. Got any fags?'

Dickie ignored him.

'That girl's not good. Still in a coma, I heard.'

'Saskia. Her name's Saskia.' He glowered at Dickie like all his troubles were Dickie's fault. 'Shit. I need to get out of here. I need to see her.'

'Like the toffs will let you anywhere near her. Even if you could. You need yer head read if you think you can waltz in and see her.'

'What if she dies? What'll happen if she dies?

'You don't even want to go there. They'll have you fer murder.

Alfie ignored him. 'So what's so important that you've come to see me? Come to gloat have you?

'If you watch yer lip I might be able to do you a favour. Just need a bit of information first. And don't tell me any bleeding lies, neither.'

'As if. So what's on yer mind?'

'First of all, did you knife that posh kid?'

'Saskia. Her name's Saskia and no I didn't. I didn't push no E's on her either. Just vodka. And hell, did she like her first taste of vodka! I had to take the bottle off her. She was well gone.'

'So where was you when the knife thing started?'

'Drinkin' with me mates. I didn't know, but that bastard pushed her in the back room. Where they keep coats and stuff. First I knew, I heard her screaming. Bastard was trying to fuck her. 'Had her dress up and everything. And had a knife at her throat. Good nine inches it was.'

'I can't see much pleasure in 'forcing' a woman. Never did force a woman.'

'No, Old Man. You had to pay for it, didn't you?'

'Nothing wrong with a little... arrangement. You'll see when you get a bit older.'

'Yeh, Right.'

'I heard your dabs was on the knife.'

'Yeh, but only 'cos I tried to stop the bastard from killing her. 'Corse it had me prints on it.'

Old Dickie made a play at digesting the facts. Thought he was a bleeding Judge. He still couldn't take his eyes of MacCarthy's missus - Alfie thought he'd get a doing over if McCarthy clocked it.

'Got a bloke what owes me a favour. He'll say he saw Ronnie Atkins attack the girl at your birthday bash. For the right sort of deal. Atkins is known fer drugs so the fuzz will put two and two together and make six. The best bit is, he left the country yesterday for a few months in Morocco.'

'Right. Except it wasn't Atkins was it? It was Zillon Osborne. Big bloke...always hanging with that runt from Reading. The one that did time last year.'

Dickie seemed to be chewing on what Alfie told him.

'Spose we could finger him then. Leave it with me. I'll get a deal set up. We'll soon have you out of 'ere. Bye the way, got any problem with pervs? Any shower shenanigans?'

.'Nothing I can't handle. Why?'

'It's just that I promised yer mother somebody on the wing would keep an eye on you. Like a son to me you are.'

'As if Old Man. As if.'

Dickie dug around in his pocket and passed a packet of twenty fags across the table. In a flash an officer was on Alfie with handcuffs at the ready.

'Get off me.' Alfie tried to flick him away. 'I haven't done nothing.'

'Don't touch a screw,' Dickie warned. 'He'll have yer.'

'Stand up Collins. Now.' A second officer appeared from nowhere. Then another. Some bastard must've called in the troops. Everybody was gawping.

'Hands behind your back.' Alfie obliged, more from panic than choice.

Dickie was ushered out and apparently you could hear him squealing as they took Alfie down to the Segregation Unit.

'Not exactly the shortest visit on record Collins, but close.' The Seg officer smiled like it was a big joke.

They put my Alfie in a cell block on the outskirts of the prison. Somewhere near the wire. He was still handcuffed. Bastards! There was no need for that. He didn't do nothing.

'First little visit to our hotel is it Collins? You'll find it very basic I'm afraid, but we do feed you.'

'Nobody told me I couldn't take smokes off an old man.'

'Well you know now.'

And that was it. He was banged up in the Block and waiting for a Governor to hand out his punishment. They

only let you out of your cell for one hour a day in
Segregation and then it's into a concrete yard. They told
him he could be staying for a week or more. It was bollocks.

Alfie chucked his supper in the sink. Said it wasn't fit for a
dog. Next day he could hear the officer outside jingling the
keys before he was unlocked and told the Governor wanted
to see him. He got marched down the corridor and shoved
in an office. Told to stand next to a desk.

'Name and number.'

'Collins. SD10943 AN.' He'd learnt that quick.

The Governor was a she-cat. Quite curvy but eyes that cut
through you. A nurse appeared and sat next to Alfie. An
officer told him to sit.

'Are the IMB coming?' the Governor asked an officer.

'No one is expected Governor.'

'Is Mr Collins fit for this adjudication, Nurse?'

'Yes Governor. Fit and well.'

Alfie looked at her and wondered how she knew if he was
fit or not. He'd never seen her before.

'Collins,' the she-cat said, checking Alfie's notes. 'What
made you think a visitor could pass things across in the
Visit's Hall? You know the rules. They're up on the walls for
everybody to read'

'No Miss. I never knew. Why can't an old bloke give me
some smokes?'

'I ask the questions Collins. Got it?'

'Yes Miss.'

'It says on your records you were given a copy of rules and
regulations in Reception. When you came in. Is that right?'

'Could've been Miss. I haven't read nothing yet. Only been
in a week Miss. Me paperwork's still in me locker.'

'Ignorance of the rules is no excuse.'

'No Miss.'

'Officer Etchins, could you read Mr Collin's Wing Report
please?

'Yes Governor. At fourteen fifty-five yesterday, Mr Collins
was seen receiving a package from a visitor in the Visits

Hall. It was passed across the table to him and he proceeded to place the package in his pocket. He was arrested and brought to Segregation. The package in question was a pack of twenty Rothman cigarettes. The Visitor was strip-searched on his way out of the Visitor's Hall but found to be carrying no other illegal items. Collins has been compliant since arrival and there are no previous nickings.'

'Do you understand the charge Mr.Collins?

'Yes Miss.'

'And how do you plead to the charge Mr.Collins?'

'Guilty I 'spose Miss but I never knew it was wrong.'

'Can you read Collins?'

'A bit Miss.'

'Have you been made aware that there are prisoners on the wing who can help you read information and write letters?'

'No Miss.'

'Think hard before you answer my next question Mr. Collins. I'll ask you again. Have you been made aware that there are prisoners on the wing who can help you read information and write letters?'

'No Miss.'

'Officer Hanks, could you find out who was on duty when Mr Collins arrived and let me know.'

'Yes Governor.'

'Mr Collins. Because you pleaded guilty and you are in prison for the first time, I am prepared to give you the benefit of the doubt. Just for the record, you never pass anything between you and your visitors. Got it?'

'Yes Miss.'

'However, you cannot go unpunished.' She stopped talking; it was like those games shows where they keep you waiting for the answers. She wrote something on a piece of paper.

'OK Mr Collins. This is what I'm going to do. You'll get three days loss of canteen and you can return to the wing.

Think yourself lucky you're not on closed visits for the next few months. And don't take me for a soft touch 'cos if you're up again, you won't be so lucky. Got it?

'Yes Miss.'

'And you do know that this prison becomes a non-smoking establishment next Monday, don't you?'

'No Miss.'

'Well you can take my word for it. Better get to see a doctor and get some nicotine patches.'

'Yes Miss.'

Canteen was the only good thing in there. You could buy extra food and soap and stuff from the canteen. And his smokes were gone, too.

'Shall I take him back to the wing Governor? Have you done?'

'More than done, Officer. How many more this morning?'

'Six Governor.'

'Let's get on, then.'

Officer Hanks took my Alfie back to his cell.

'Hand over your smokes Collins.' The screw watched as he dug them out of his locker.

'All of 'em.'

'That's it Sir. Have a look. See? The screw checked his cell and then walked out with his ciggies. He was laughing, the bastard.

A bit later his cell door opened again.

'Here's your paperwork Collins. Make sure you read it this time.'

'I want to make a complaint.'

'Yeah, yeah. Everybody wants to complain about this place. Shut yer rattle and learn to follow the rules. That's good advice mate. Get it in your thick skull and things will go better for you.'

Alfie didn't answer. He sat on his metal bed and stared at the bog and decided then and there he was definitely going to cut himself before the trial.

Lottie

I took Maddie Frost to see Saskia to ensure she knew who I was agonising over. I wanted her to see Saskia as a living, breathing young woman rather than someone whose interests could be disregarded. Sister offered us a small office for our meeting and I led Maddie into the cramped, windowless room.

'Have the medical team given you any indication when Saskia may wake up?'

'The most hope we have is there doesn't appear to be any brain damage. And her abdominal wound is healing well. She's scarred, but it's healed OK.'

'I know very little about comas but I guess they can last a fair while.'

'Umm....she could stay asleep right up until the baby is born. If that happens, natural childbirth would be unusual, although it has been documented. The more likely route would be a C section about four weeks before her due date.'

'What does your heart tell you Lottie? Have you any idea what Saskia would want?'

'I only know what she wouldn't want. She was illegitimate and we adopted her when she was two. I think she'd want to give this baby the same chance she had. Not to be scraped away before it has the chance to live.'

'And if you're wrong? If she wakes up when she's seven months and doesn't want it?'

'Then we'll deal with it. Better that than she wakes up to find we've flipped a little life down the loo, don't you think?'

'You sound passionate about this Lottie. Is there any underlying issue that makes you feel so strongly?'

'I think I'm being a decent human being and I'll make no apologies for that.'

There was a knock on the door and a nurse asked if we'd like a cup of tea. What a life-saver. I could feel a wobble coming on and it wouldn't have looked very grown up if I'd cried.

We talked some more about the legality of the situation.

'We could have Saskia made a ward of court to protect her interests, if we think you and Tom aren't able to do so; if you stay opposed to each other's stance.'

I absorbed that snippet of information. It felt like blackmail to make one of us capitulate but it also swung things in my favour.

'I don't think it will come to that. We need to talk some more and see if we can find some common ground.' I imagined Tom's face when I told him the decision could be taken out of our hands if he insisted on an abortion. I felt I had already won.

Mummy, there are some things you should know....Alfie and me...we've been...doing it, you know. Having sex. He was careful not to push me 'cos he knew I'd not done it before. But I was ready and....I liked it. He was so gentle and we're in love...If you knew him Mummy, really took the time to know him... I'm sure you'd like him.

The weeks slipped by and Saskia still held on to her baby. I don't remember Tom and I discussing it again. There was acquiescence on his part and quiet jubilation on mine. I knew he would never allow a court case to decide our daughter's future and surely common sense told him he couldn't win.

The day of the trial loomed and no one was ready for it. Tom and I had fallen into a rhythm of barely speaking and certainly any scant conversation we had never moved far from 'steak or fish'. Looking back, I don't believe we had the mental or emotional resources to deal with our marriage, but maybe we should have found some

Tom decided to mow the lawns the day before the court case and I should have joined him in the garden to keep my mind off things. He was good at diverting his thoughts into something more useful than speculation, while I stressed over a mug of mint tea and stared into space. Enid had gone home and the boys were away which left the house with an unsettling calm. The silence propagated my fears.

I watched the man I probably still loved stride across the grass with intent; up then down he walked creating a monotonous rhythm. The smell of new-mown grass wafted through the window and the gentle hum of the mower should have soothed me, but it didn't. I couldn't imagine feeling soothed until Saskia woke. I saw the stripes on the lawn multiply with Tom's mechanical effort and submerged a desire to count them.

I decided to make a cottage pie for supper. At least it got me off the kitchen stool and away from my cold cup of mint tea. I thought we would both appreciate comfort food on the eve of the trial. The onions made a satisfying sizzle and I watched the meat cook as it changed from red to brown in the frying pan. The pungent aroma reminded me of childhood days when I watched Mum get supper at the farm. We didn't get many chances to eat cottage pie at Churchill's because life led us down a more sophisticated culinary route. But it was one of Saskia's favourite meals and as I thought about her, I convinced myself it was the onions making me cry. The gin bottle was on standby.

When I thought about the nitty gritty of the procedure ahead of us, I could hardly comprehend how I would listen to days and days of evidence. It would be a blood-bath on the senses and I knew I wasn't ready to hear about the misdemeanours of my daughter. And it was all due for public consumption because that little shit wouldn't plead guilty

I knew I had to tell both my parents about Saskia's involvement with drugs but it had been easier to shelve the decision until 'later'. However, when it was agreed they would attend court, I knew they'd hear all the gory detail from someone else's mouth. Tom said I should have told them weeks before and he'd even offered to do it for me, but it would have been cowardly to duck the responsibility. Consequently I did it at the eleventh hour.

My parents idolised Saskia and I didn't want her tarnished in their eyes. From the day she arrived as a cheeky toddler they had embraced her as family. They'd watched her grow with unbridled pride and during her schooling at Cheltenham a deeper relationship with her had blossomed. But I needn't have worried. Dad's response was as cool as you like. 'You hear it all the time with those agricultural students,' he said. 'Drugs are everywhere aren't they?' It was a huge relief when they both took it so well but how on earth they would cope with all the other things they were going to be exposed to, I had no idea.

I'd never been to a court case before, but on television programmes I'd noticed everyone dressed smartly and in sober mode. It was easy for Tom, as any one of his work suits was suitable. I decided on my grey linen slacks which I was delighted to find were baggy and required a belt, a white blouse and no jewellery. I added a navy blazer as an option if the weather turned cooler. Everything was a blur and I had the attention span of a gnat.

We'd decided Tom would be the one to give evidence while I would sit in court with Mum or Dad. Tom said he would visit Saskia while I was in court and I would see her when court was over for the day. I pondered the possibility that she would wake on the very first day of the trial and tell the court all about bloody Alfie Collins. But I knew the chances of that happening were only slightly higher than nil.

'Any chance of coffee Snooks? It's hot as hell out there.'

Tom appeared in the kitchen and I hadn't even notice the silence of the mower. 'Sure. Let me wash the onion off my hands and I'll join you.' We sat by the window, each waiting for the other to speak.

'The hollyhocks have done well this year. They need a bit of weeding but they're a good six feet.'

I should have responded with an offer to weed, but I didn't.

'The gold price has gone up two percent today. Did you see the article in The Times? Good investment so far.'

Like I'd read the bloody paper and did I care a shit about the price of gold? Instead, I wanted to yell at him that Saskia's baby was not going anywhere until it was ready to enter the world through normal channels, but I didn't.

'It's lovely outside Darling. Fancy a bit of weeding?' Tom asked.

'I'm making cottage pie. Bit busy.'

'Thought I could smell something nice. Well I'd better get on. Thanks for the coffee.'

I watched him stride back to his lawnmower and I tried to recall those happy student days when he made my pulse race. But I couldn't. I tried to think of all the things we hadn't said to each other since Saskia slipped into a coma, but I couldn't manage that either.

The phone rang and it was Dad to tell me he'd be with us by eight o'clock the next morning. I told him I'd have something nice for him to eat.

'Not a bad idea. Get something in the belly. An army marches on its belly,' he chuckled.

I smiled and realised I couldn't wait to see him. I needed his reassurance; I needed a hug and more than anything, I needed his support to see me through this ordeal. I intended to keep the news of the baby to myself for a while. There would be plenty of time for that conversation when Collins was sent to prison.

Dad had always been a stalwart with his down-to-earth logic and it was good to know he'd be there. He'd stop me killing bloody Alfie Collins with my bare hands which was a bonus. I wanted to smell that earthy scent of tweed jacket and see him remove his cap to expose a bald pate which was the only hairstyle I could ever remember. I wanted to be his little girl again.

The next day we woke to wall to wall sunshine and no blazer was required. I'd promised Dad food when he arrived around eight and a full English breakfast fitted the bill. Enid had made sure everything was in the fridge to meet the demands of the largest appetite and I'd part-cooked the sausages while the bacon lay in limp, pink strips in readiness for the grill. I was expecting Tom to join Dad for breakfast although I didn't ask him if he was hungry. I would probably only manage to toy with a piece of toast.

I saw Dad's Landrover come through our gates and a flutter of excitement made my heart race. I rushed to meet him while Tom took a more leisurely approach as he crossed the hall to open the door. I shot through the doorway to reach my Dad and shrieked with delight.

'Lottie Lottie drives me potty.' He called as he locked his car and opened his arms as wide as a field gate.

'How's my lovely girl?' he asked as he swept me off my feet. You're a bit on the light side love. You need a bit of meat on those bones.'

I buried my face in the scent of him, just as I did as a child and wondered if I was using regression to cope with the stress. If that was the case, Nancy would be impressed by my self-awareness. I caught a shadow of disapproval from Tom which disappeared as quickly as it appeared. He was probably pleased no boys were around to witness my overt display of emotion. But I didn't care. I let the flow of love wash over me and wallowed in the arms of my dad.

Tom waited until Dad released me and then shook him by the hand. 'Welcome Eric. It seems too long since you were here. How's Stella?'

'Oh, you know. Well as can be expected, apart from the odd aches and pains. And... this of course. This coma thing has taken the stuffing out of us both.'

'Let's go inside. Lottie has a breakfast banquet prepared.'

I selfishly wanted a few minutes of Dad all to myself but that didn't happen. So I busied myself in the kitchen while Tom and Dad talked dairy herds and gardens.

'I hope you're joining us my girl, I see there's only two places laid for this feast.'

I glanced at the kitchen table and felt a flush of guilt that I wasn't even having a bacon sandwich and I knew an effort on my part would please both men in my life. 'I'll eat tonight. And I'll have some toast now.'

'No wonder you're like a rasher of wind. If you stand sideways, I can't see you.'

Dad smiled but his smile didn't quite reach his eyes. I knew he was worried about me but I couldn't take on any more responsibility.

Tom made the coffee and I buttered fresh bread for Dad to dip in his egg.

'One egg or two, boys?'

A chorus of 'two' sailed back and I wondered why men could fill their bellies in the face of conflict when women took a more apprehensive approach. I sat and kept the conversation flowing, hoping they would forget to watch how little I ate. I wished I had a greedy Labrador at my feet to eat my unwanted breakfast.

As Tom was to be a witness for the prosecution, he was barred from the proceedings until after he'd given evidence. He looked like a lost little boy when Dad and I departed for court.

'Good luck Snooks. I'll be with you every step of the way. Remember that.'

'Give Saskia a big hug and tell her I'll be in later.' I kissed him. I was sad Dad had to go straight home after the hearing as I knew he wanted to see Saskia, too. Tom promised to pick me up from the court when the day was done.

'And remember he's not worthy of your anger. He's nothing but a worm under your shoe, so how can he upset you?'

Hmm...I wasn't sure I could follow that logic where Alfie Collins was concerned. Father of my grandchild sprang into my head, but I put on a brave face. As Dad and I swept out of the driveway that morning, I caught a smile from Tom which was meant to give me confidence to face the day.

And maybe I saw regret that we'd rowed so badly in recent days. He'd told me the nightmare would soon be over and I prayed he was right.

We were met on the court steps not only by a barrage of reporters and cameras, but also a police family liaison officer called Karen who had called on us a couple of times. Dad was almost frozen with fear by the scrum and I heard myself encouraging him to get inside.

'It's ghastly isn't it? Karen looked calm and had probably seen it all before. 'Try to think of the benefits they offer when they get the story right.'

I'd made a point of not reading the papers for weeks and I couldn't imagine I would read the court reports either. I introduced Dad and we were ushered into the court room where seats were found for us.

'I'm not staying for the hearing but I'll come back at lunchtime to make sure you're OK.' Karen was carrying a bulging briefcase and had the look of a busy woman.

I thanked her and absorbed the alien world. I looked at the long polished benches which I guessed were for the jury and I stared at the dock. I knew from the moment Alfie Collins entered the court room he would become real; he'd be etched on my mind for the rest of my life. No longer a faceless hooligan, he'd be a criminal, a man who nearly killed our daughter. I'd endured months of Alfie Collins festering in my brain and I was a shadow of the woman I wanted to be. Instead I was the woman who took comfort from stabbing a voodoo doll with Saskia's school compass. I actually enjoyed sticking barbs into a faceless yob and laying blame; I vented my anger on a faceless ruffian from a sink-estate family. But I knew it was too easy to hide behind a safety blanket of ignorance, to fall into denial about Saskia's culpability. She must, undoubtedly, take a portion of blame.

I looked around as the court filled up and wondered about the jury; they'd be ordinary people I could have seen in Waitrose. Dad took my hand which made me want to cry.

How ridiculous was that? I knew the blanket of anonymity was about to be whipped away like a layer of skin, but I didn't feel ready. Collins would be there in the flesh in a couple of minutes; his eyes, his hair and his skin would be forever tattooed on my brain. We'd breathe the same air. I'd shroud him in my cloud of anger and when I looked him in the eye, he'd know I hated him. But that wouldn't hurt him would it? The worst thing of all was having no idea how I'd ever move on from this experience because hate has no healing qualities.

And it wasn't only me who was racked with fear; that morning Tom had paced while drinking his morning coffee and was short with me over bathroom preferences. But he, of course, was true to tradition and mustered a strategy to deal with the day. He seemed to cope with anything life threw his way and I decided, not for the first time, that coping was probably written into his DNA. Tom lived on a cerebral plane which, at that moment, appeared so much more attractive than my lot in life, particularly while I was perched with my Dad on this emotional slag-heap. I made a note to try harder.

In my mind it was a no-brainer that Collins would be found guilty and it was the only verdict I'd considered. I longed for Saskia to wake because maybe, just maybe, that would soften my stance towards Alfie Collins. I didn't want to carry so much hate around because it was like a sack of rocks on my shoulders and I was bowed with the burden. But still my daughter lay in silent repose, offering no more than the occasional flutter of her eyelids.

The one bright spot in my life, I realised as I waited for the court case to get under way, was that I'd managed to keep Saskia's baby cradled in her womb. Through my cajoling and long silences, Tom hadn't found the courage to insist upon an abortion. And I'd been sneaky. I'd left nothing to chance.

A few days before the court hearing, I'd sourced a specialist charity who gave me impartial advice about our situation. I was able to raise all my issues such as conception from rape and what Saskia's wishes might be if she wasn't in a coma. But was it rape? I liked to imagine it was, but I couldn't erase the memory of how happy my daughter was during those weeks when she must have been meeting Collins. Facing unattractive truths was stressful and it was the imagined detail teased from the knot of turmoil that crippled me. I was grateful to the anonymous lady who listened to my grief. She'd gently steered the conversation to deal with what I knew, rather than those things I supposed to be true. And rights of the unborn child gave me hope. I knew about the problems facing medical staff when two parents had polar opinions and from what I'd read, common sense usually prevailed. Alleluia.

Tracey

I'd had to cancel work 'cos of going to court and had no idea what we'd live on. It could have gone on for a week or more but I had to be there for Alfie. I needed extra allowances to see me over the court case which meant queuing down the job centre and telling some stranger all our family business.

Mum said she'd have Lily while I was in court, which was a first.

'I'll give her a bit of dinner,' she said. You pick her up when yer ready love. We'll probably go to the park most days.'

Just my luck the court case cropped up in school holidays. But I had no idea what had got into me mother.

'That lad of yours will probably get what's coming to him.' She pursed her lips like a pantomime dame. 'Can't see him getting away with it.'

She thought she was bloody mystic Meg, my mother. *'That lad of yours?'* Hmm...Whatever happened to *'my grandson?'* She sounded like she'd already disowned Alfie. And as if I didn't know what was gonna happen to my boy. I didn't need reminding.

I'd told Lily about her brother. It wasn't easy, but I had to do it before some kid told her about all the shenanigans. Kids do a lot of earwigging into adult conversations so I had to tell her he might go to prison. She cried and bit and wanted to know what it would be like in there. And she said she wanted to visit, but I wasn't sure about that. Prison wasn't any place for my Lily.

I heard a key in the door and me stomach flipped 'cos for one second, I thought it might be Alfie. Quick enough I realised it was Dickie.

'All right are you Ducks?'

'What do you think?'

'Now now. No good looking on the black side. He might get off.'

'Cows might bleeding fly.'

He settled himself on me sofa without asking. 'Need any help with Lily? Like me to come to court with you?'

I shook me head. 'I'm OK on me own.

'Sure you are Ducks. Never let anybody close, do you?'

'All them years on the game, I expect. Ring any bells?' I looked at him like thunder and wished he'd piss off out of our lives. I knew he never would. They'd take him out of Skankland in a box.

'I've got to get down the social to see about some money to cover the court case. Could go on for days. Shan't be able to work.'

'I'd give the food bank a ring. That's just the sort of thing they're there for. 'Why ain't you giving evidence?'

'No need. That do-gooder from the youth club offered. Seems she thinks Alfie's a 'talented man'. Yeh right. Don't take talent to get put inside.'

'Must say I'm a bit surprised.'

'What? That I'm not giving evidence? She'll do a better job than me. I'd get all tongue-tied with nerves if they put me in the witness box.'

'Your trouble is you always look on the dark side of life, Trace.'

'P'raps that's cos it's the only side I know. Anyway, I gotta get on. See yerself out.'

As I walked to the bus stop I wondered what my Alfie was thinking. How was he feeling? Hours and hours locked in a cell made time for a lot of thinking. He must have known he would probably go down although he could be pretty cocky when he wanted.

Trouble never seemed to leave my doorstep. I'd had a phone call from the screws a few days before to say they'd moved Alfie onto a different wing 'cos the silly bugger had cut his wrists. I nearly wet meself when they told me. I couldn't believe Alfie would be so stupid. He's not the type. Then the penny dropped and I realised what his 'slicer' was for. I imagined all sorts of awful things and wondered if it was bad enough for me to lose my boy.

I went to see him the next day in the hospital wing and the little bugger had a grin on his face from ear to ear. And there was me thinking he was at death's door. I couldn't have a go at him with all the screws about, but I wanted to clip his ear. Apparently, he never meant to kill himself, it was all a bit of shenanigans. He'd been told they'd move him to the vulnerable prisoner's wing if he tried to cut himself. Apparently life was a bit less violent in there.

I was mighty relieved when I found out the truth of the matter, but I'd still have had a go at him for being so stupid. What if it had gone wrong? Trouble was, he had such a way with him it was hard to be angry for long. Sometimes, I thought Alfie could have made it in the movies with a bit of a break. Face of an angel, Annie Etheridge always said. Girls couldn't resist him, even that posh girl who was no better than the slappers round our way, went with him. What sort of parent lets a sixteen year old girl out to mix with booze and drugs?

There was the usual queue at the social and I stood next to a woman who smelled like a polecat. I can't stand dirty people and I let the bloke behind me go in front.

'Thanks love.' When I looked at him he winked and I knew I'd seen him before. I was trying to work out where I knew him from when he touched my arm.

'Did you ever go back and get your GCSE's Trace?'

It was the voice, I think, that gave him away. 'Alan Curtis? Bloody hell. Thought you went in the army.'

'I did, but I'm out now. Did fifteen years. That was enough. What you been up to. How's your Alfie?'

Where to start? I couldn't think of anything to say and the next thing I knew I was crying. Not a little sniff, but a flood of snot and tears that seemed to come from nowhere.

'Hey Trace. No need for that, is there?'

He put an arm round me shoulder which made matters worse.

'Move up love. Yer holding up the queue.' A miserable old git three behind me started fussing.

'Do you mind? Can't you see the lady's upset?'

'Tears won't pay my phone bill nor buy me ciggies.'

'She don't look like a lady from where I'm standing.'

Alan looked like he might clobber a red-headed bloke who was mouthing off, but the next thing I knew he got hold of me and we were out the door.

'I gotta get some money....I need.....'

'You don't need nothing if you're a friend of Alan Curtis, Trace. Come on.'

I sat in his car and kept crying. It felt like I'd never stop. 'I'm not a baby, honest.'

'Gutsy more like. You were always gutsy. Keeping your Alfie was gutsy.'

I kept hearing the word gutsy in me head. Gutsy...gutsy...it was going round and round like a tumble dryer.

'Look after his mum does young Alfie? What's he now – seventeen, eighteen?'

I cried a bit more but I didn't tell him about my Alfie. And I didn't tell him about Lily neither.

I told him I didn't want him to do it...the man who gave me the ciggy. He kept trying...but I said no. Honest Mummy. I said no but I don't think he heard me. Then he got a knife from somewhere...and...his other hand was up my skirt. Mummy I was petrified. I don't know if he did anything to me...

Lottie

I was still waiting for something to happen while Dad looked around the court room as if he'd been dropped on Mars.

'Did Mum get her dentures sorted? She was really stressing about them when I spoke to her.'

Dad chuckled. 'She did. What she was stressing about was going to WI without them. You know she cares what everybody thinks. Bugger if I'd care, but your Mum's different. You know that.'

Butterflies had infested my body, or I wondered if those moths from Europe had taken a liking to my insides. I allowed my eyes to focus on the empty jury seats and guessed the judge would appear from the central door on the panelled wood wall. The craftsmanship from years gone by was amazing and I wondered how long it would be before it was ripped out in the name of progress.

Seats filled up around us and the buzz of conversation reminded me of waiting for a Christmas pantomime to begin. Mum always took me to Cheltenham to see the pantomimes when I was a child and I loved the sequins and the rude jokes. But I was always nervous while we waited for it to start. I thought we might have come on the wrong day or maybe it was cancelled. Silly child! One thing was certain about the court case, it wouldn't be cancelled and there'd be no jokes.

The reporters were chatting amongst themselves and I wondered if the case would be in the Wilts and Glos. I decided it was unlikely, unless any reporters twigged my home town was Cirencester. Someone told me they liked to do that sort of thing; it earned Brownie points if they tipped off a colleague about a person's connection to another area. I hoped for Mum and Dad's sakes they wouldn't make the connection.

I tried to guess where the little shit's family were sitting and realised if they were behind me, then I had no chance to identify them. Either his mother or father must be black, but I could see only white people around me.

Suddenly the court was told to rise and I tried to still my heartbeat. My mouth was desiccated but my hands were slicked with sweat. How does that work? But before I found an answer to the workings of my body, there was a shuffling around me which suggested the event about to unfold. The judge bowed and took her seat on a raised dais while the jury filed into their seats in an orderly line. It was impossible to guess characters or dispositions from their appearance, but I prayed they would deliver the right verdict.

Then *he* arrived - my nemesis. A yob by the name of Alfie Collins rose from steps behind the dock and I was riveted by his appearance. He wore a smart grey suit with a blue polka-dot tie and his glossy hair was brushed to perfection. There was a male officer beside him but he wasn't handcuffed although he looked scared, which I found oddly comforting. His black hair sat on his collar and had a gentle curl any girl would be proud of; his skin was a pale, milk chocolate. I noticed he was tall and broad-shouldered as he stood in the dock and.... I grudgingly had to admit he was attractive. A small, mousy woman on the end of our row started to cry when he appeared but she didn't look old enough to be his mother.

The prosecution laid before us a scenario of which much was surmised. No one could know the full truth until my baby woke up. I heard sentences such as 'and can a young innocent girl from a good family take the blame for ending up at a drug-fuelled party?'

Of course she can't. No, that was my fault.
'The prosecution witness will say she was coerced to attend a party by the man you see in the dock ladies and gentlemen of the jury. This is the man who was heard to threaten her with a knife, before stabbing her.'

This was already too much to bear and I had no idea how I'd cope with the coming days. I wished I'd brought a bottle of water. Dad squeezed my hand which nearly brought a cloud-burst of tears and all I could think of was how scared Saskia must have been. The barrister's voice continued like a bee in a jam jar.

'You will hear how this same man was seen leaving the scene wearing blood stained clothing. You will hear how his finger prints were found on the knife. And you will hear how the young girl is still in a coma, caused by the consumption of drugs and injuries the prosecution witness will say was inflicted by this man.'

I zoned out. It was an ability I'd learned years before but it could catch me out when I missed chunks of conversation. Sometimes, it saved me from things I didn't want to hear.

They called the caretaker of the premises to give evidence and he confirmed what I already knew. Alfie bloody Collins was to blame. He told the court that alcohol and drugs were forbidden on the premises, so why, I whispered to Dad, didn't he do his job and keep my Saskia safe? He said he saw blood on Saskia's clothing and he saw the knife. I felt crumpled by the words floating around the court.

I noticed people pouring coffee from flasks as if they were there for the spectacle and a young lad was texting on his phone which was supposed to be switched off. It seemed that life continued all around us for everyone else, but not for Dad and me. I felt stranded in a bubble while I waited for justice to be carried out.

The jury were attentive. I wondered what they did for a living and if any had a sixteen year old daughter who'd deceived them. Of course they hadn't.

Lunch was a sandwich more suited to feeding ducks. Dad and I hardly referred to the hearing while we munched, preferring to malign the meagre content of our sandwiches. Karen didn't show, but I didn't care. I watched all those people who didn't have a child lying in a coma and envied them their freedom from the misery that was ours. The coffee shop failed dismally to satisfy my need for a strong gin and tonic; instead we made do with well-stewed tea which Dad loaded with sugar because Mum wasn't there to stop him.

Dad and I took our seats for the afternoon session and the proceedings dragged on with little else of note revealed. A member of the jury nodded off around three o'clock; he was probably a victim of the stifling heat. I watched the smart lady next to him poke him awake, which would have been amusing on any other occasion.

Eventually, I joined Tom who was waiting outside in the car, as arranged, and before I was ready to say goodbye to him, Dad kissed me and wished us luck. He confirmed Mum was on her way and needed to be met off the seven o'clock train.

'How was it Snooks? You looked bushed.' Tom put his hand on my shoulder. I had no idea how I was but I didn't want to fall into his arms. I wanted my dad. I must have offered some platitude to satisfy my husband.

'Saw a lot of people coming out. Was the court full?'

'It was. And so hot. I must remember to take water tomorrow.'

'Was Eric OK? Don't expect it was easy for him hear the evidence.'

'He was a stalwart. The only problem was his bladder. I'm wondering if he's got prostate problems. Bless him. It was almost funny to see him squeeze along the row so many times. And so full of apologies.'

'Do you think they'll nail him? Collins?'

'It's too early to say, but there's plenty of evidence against him.'

'What did you think of him?'

'I expected a tough looking yob and saw a prospective lawyer. He was so spruced up it was a shock.'

'Easy to put on a suit Darling, but it doesn't make him any less guilty, does it?'

'How was Saskia?'

'Fragrant. They'd bathed her and she looked beautiful. Shall we pick Mum and up then go straight to see her? We could eat out.'

'Good idea.' To be honest, I had no idea how food entered Tom's head, but I was happy to push a few bits around a plate and Mum might be hungry.

The train was fifteen minutes late and Mum was flustered because she'd caused us 'inconvenience'.

'It's not a problem Mum. Honestly. How was the journey?'

I gave her a hug but it didn't ooze the essence of revival I'd got from my Dad.

Our daughter was in her pink tracksuit bottoms and a white tee-shirt announcing 'Live a Little' in gold letters. The irony was not lost on us. I had clean clothes for her and I changed her socks for her favourite Micky Mouse pair. When I'd finished, Mum and I sat either side of her and Mum tentatively held her hand. I noticed the incongruity of the old skin entwined with the perfect skin.

I didn't tell Saskia I'd been to court and had my first siting of the monster who'd damaged her; I told her we were going to take our holiday in Scilly when she woke. Hurry up, I urged her. I reminded her of the walk around the Garrison and the pasties at the Turk's head on St Agnes. When she was little, the St. Mary's boatmen used to let her steer their boats. Frazer was the most fun and he'd tease her about being the first woman boatman in Scilly. Hmm... hell would freeze over before that happened. They didn't even recognise the word 'boatperson' on the islands!

I felt drained and we only stayed with our daughter for a short while. I kissed her and told her we'd be in again the next day.

'Shall we try Pizza Express Snooks?'

I was shocked at Tom's suggestion; I was sure he'd never graced a Pizza Express in his life. 'Fine. Is it OK with you Mum? Pizza? It should be quick at this time and no college boys around either.' I wasn't fussed what we ate and Mum seemed happy to eat anything, too.

Over supper Mum announced that she intended to stay until the trial was over. Apparently, it was all arranged and a neighbour was going to keep an eye on Dad. She'd made sure there was enough to eat in the freezer and given Dad a lesson on how the use the microwave. It was going to be a mixed blessing for me as I had no spare emotional capacity to give her.

When we got home Mum wanted to unpack her things and have an early night. I kissed her after making sure she had a glass of water to take her pills. 'Sleep well.'

'I always do love. Only the wicked can't sleep!'

When I went into the drawing room Tom had already poured me a gin and tonic. 'I had no idea she'd stay so long.' I gulped at my gin. 'I'm not sure I can cope with Mum as well as everything else.' I felt near to tears which I put down to the emotion of the day.

'She wants to look after you. We all do. Let us both spoil you for a change.'

I wished my dad was with me, but he wasn't and I needed to buck up and find the strength to see me through the next few weeks.

Over our cocktails Tom told me he'd picked up bits of gossip from Enid who apparently lived close to Alfie Collin's grandmother. Enid told Tom there was no father on the scene and the mother was little more than a child when she had him. So it could have been her sitting on the end of the row. How grim.

Tracey

Just as I finished ironing Lily's school uniform, which she wouldn't need for a few weeks, there was a knock at the door. I hoped it wasn't Dickie come to have another go at me. I needed time to think about it all, to weigh up the pros and cons before getting knee-deep in something I had no control over. I'd done that too many times in my life. But Lily answered it before I had time to think and then came into the kitchen with a funny look on her face.

'Mum, it's a man.

She scarpered past me to go back to her tele programme.

'Hiya Trace. Can I come in a minute?'

I was a bit taken aback to be honest. How did Alan Curtis find out where I lived? I stood aside and he came right in to the sitting room.

'Hello. And who are you then?'

'I'm Lily. Do you like The Simpsons?'

'I do. I've come to have a chat with yer Mum.'

I nodded him into the kitchen. 'Tea?'

'That would be good, Trace.'

I put the kettle on and tried to get a quick look at him as he sat down.

'How long you been here then?'

'Too bloody long. Where you living?'

'My Gramps left me a small house in Durnford Road when he died about five years

ago. I've been letting it out until I finished in the army. I'm with Mum for another couple of weeks, then I move in.'

'Blimey. You did alright.'

'I loved the old man, Trace. He always told me I'd get the house when he died. Not sure I thought much about it 'til he went. It's nothing posh, but I'm lucky. Lucky to have my own place.'

I swilled the tea bags round the mugs and slopped milk in. Alan got up and carried them all of four feet to the table.

'What you doing for a job now yer out?'

'Had a bit of luck, there.' He slurped his tea which must have been scolding hot. 'I start at Reynolds Transport on the industrial estate in three weeks' time. I learned a trade in the army and I'm lucky…. picking up a job so quick. Got a foreman's job.'

I wondered why he'd come, but it seemed a bit rude to ask.

'What you up to then Trace? I heard about your Alfie from Mum. Is that what all the tears were about the other day? Why didn't you tell me?'

I didn't know what to say. 'Might have been. Not sure I know, really.'

I remembered Alan used to have a stutter and everyone used to tease him. I wanted to ask about his stutter but that seemed rude, too.

After we'd drunk the tea and caught up a bit, he dug around in his pocket like he'd lost his hankie.

'Here. This'll tide you over.'

It was an open envelope and it was stuffed with notes.

'It's five hundred quid Trace and I don't want it back.'

I pushed the envelope across the table. 'I ain't a charity case.'

'Never said you were, but everybody needs a leg up at one time or another. Are you
telling me you can manage? Course you can't.'

No, I bloody well couldn't but I knew what would come next. As Mum always said, *'there's no such thing as a free dinner.'*

Alan got up and put the kettle on again. 'I'll take you for a pint tonight, if you fancy it.'

He made us another brew, and moved round my kitchen like he'd been there before.

'Can't. I've got Lily.'

'How about we go to the Plough on Sunday then? All of us. Have a bit of dinner? The play area's good there for little kids.'

What was it with him? He never took any notice of me when we were at school and I hadn't improved with keeping. I knew the Plough was posh. I pretended to think about it but really I was wondering if I had something to wear. 'Alright then. I can't pay and you ain't getting nothing else. No funny business. Understood?'

He actually laughed at me like I was funny.

'Still feisty then Trace? I'll be paying, you and Lily will be eating and no funny business, as you put it. I'll pick you up at twelve.'

He got up and he was still chuckling. I watched to see if he picked up the envelope with the money in it.

'Tell you what Trace, you use this as a leg up and pay me back if you can. OK?'

I nodded. I stood at the kitchen window and watched his car disappear. I couldn't help a little smile. 'Lily, we're going out proper posh on Sunday.'

By Sunday I was feeling a bit sick. I couldn't remember when a bloke had taken me out and there had never been one to take my Lily as well. I was wondering what the catch was going to be.

'Can I wear my princess dress Mum?'

I had to think about it 'cos I had no idea what people wore out for Sunday dinner. I told her it would be fine. It was one less thing to worry about. I changed my own outfit about four times and I still didn't know what to wear. It was warm so I didn't need a coat which was lucky 'cos I only had an old mac or my hoodie. I'd been to a charity shop and found a dress with a tie belt which I hoped flattered me figure, without being showy

I noticed in the mirror that a few days of sun had brought out me freckles but it couldn't be helped. I'd raided Mum's makeup when I fetched Lily on Friday and used her concealer and pink lipstick. I'd got my own mascara and I reckoned that was all I needed. Lily had given me some cheap perfume for me birthday, so a squirt of that boosted me confidence a bit. It was a funny feeling, having a bloke take an interest in me when it wasn't for sex. I could get to like it.

Lily looked fantastic. She was as pretty as a picture and she handed me her hairbrush with instruction that she wasn't having plaits and she wasn't having a ponytail.

'Too much like school. Did you ever see a princess with plaits?'

'No. I don't believe I did.'

I brushed her soft blonde hair until it shone and persuaded her that princesses wore Alice bands. She has really happy and kept getting in my way when I tried to use the mirror.

'Sit and watch tele so you don't get dirty.'

'CBeebie's is boring. Can I watch a DVD?'

Anything was OK as long as she gave me a bit of peace to get ready.

I'd been thinking about Alan Curtis off and on. I asked Mum what she knew about him and she hadn't heard anything for years. She knew his Gramp died, but nothing else. Part of me didn't think I should go out with him while my Alfie was locked up. But it was a real treat for Lily so I was swayed. I told her I wanted best behaviour and she asked if Alan was my boyfriend. I told her I didn't want to hear such nonsense.

I watched Alan park his car and decided he wasn't half bad. The day I'd snivelled all over him, I hadn't got a proper look and I'd felt shy when he plonked himself in my kitchen so didn't dare do much looking. But he was tall; he must have been six foot. And smart, too. He'd got nice jeans on and a black shirt. His hair was short and you could have guessed he'd been in the army.

He knocked on the door.

'I'll go. I'll go.' Lily raced to open it and I heard him admire her princess dress. 'Father Christmas gave it to me but I've never worn it outside. Only in the house.'

I smiled. She'd probably have told him her life-history, if he asked.

'Hi Trace. You look nice.'

I was a bit lost for words. 'Er... thanks. You look nice too.' What a daft thing to say to a bloke!

'I've booked a table for one o'clock so there's time to sit outside with a drink.'

'How do you book a table?' Lily was a nosey little madam. She always had to know everything.

'Well, when you take a princess and her Mum out, you need to be sure there'll be a special table for them to eat from. So you ring up and organise it, then no one else can sit there.'

'Wow. Cool.'

We both laughed and it broke the ice.

'Come on then. Your car awaits. Princesses go first.'

I suddenly wondered why he wasn't married. I'd not thought about it before but I decided he probably was. Wouldn't that be just my luck?

He was a good talker. I didn't have to say much to start with. Between him and Lily, they talked for England.

We drove to the Plough which was about three miles away. I used to think I'd like to work there when I was at school, but I never did. But if I'd had to choose between working at the Plough and having my Alfie, I'd definitely have gone for Alfie.

The carpark was nearly full, even though we were early. Lily was beside herself with excitement and kept trying to point out empty parking spaces.

'Leave it to Alan love. He'll find somewhere.'

As I let Lily out of the back seat I was suddenly nervous. My stomach churned but there was no time to think because Lily ran off shouting, 'over here. The door's over here.' I smiled at Alan who looked amused and I wondered if he'd got any kids. He seemed to have a way with them.

Alan opened the door and let us in and I told Lily to stay right next to me. Her eyes were all over the place and I wasn't much better. I was right, all those years ago – it was posh. We opened the door into a huge garden and found a bench in the shade which pleased me. The sun always made me red and blotchy. I sat down while Lily ran off to play with some children and Alan disappeared with our drinks order. I thought to myself that if I hadn't had Alfie so young, this could have been my life. I'd have had a nice bloke and enough money to eat at posh places. But I didn't have long to think about it 'cos Alan appeared with drinks and Lily came running back to claim hers.

'Look Mum. Can I go on the slide?

We watched as she tried out all the play stuff and I sipped my half of beer, smiling at her. It wasn't often we got to have fun together.

'I like this place. I've got a nipper of me own and she likes to come here. I only have her every other weekend though.'

So he had been married. And had a kid. I was tongue-tied so I never asked any questions. When we'd finished our drinks Alan said we should claim our table. I lured Lily inside with the promise of ice cream if she ate her dinner.

'The table is in the name of Curtis', he said, calm as you like.

A waitress led us to a table for four by the window.

'Someone will take your drinks order Sir.' She handed us all a menu. Even Lily got one.

Can I have anything I want?'

I gave her one of my looks and she went quiet.

'Nice place,' I said. I wished I'd put on a bit more makeup.

'Glad you like it, Trace.

I'd read in one of those trashy magazines the girls left lying around in the factory, if you're nervous on a date, always ask the bloke something about himself. So I went for it.

'Why haven't I seen you about fer years?' I lowered my eyes to the menu while he answered.

'I've been back from time to time. We just haven't seen each other. I joined the REME at sixteen and I've served overseas quite a lot.'

'What's the REME?' Lily was all bright eyed and excited so I shot her a 'good behaviour' look.

'I used to mend lorries and tanks in the army. We kept the army going,' he said with a chuckle. Seen anything you like on the menu Lily?'

'I can read now you know.'

'You look like a smart kid to me. Have you seen the children's menu on the back? Bet there's something you'd like on that.'

I was thinking he was too good to be true and waited for the bomb-shell. 'So what did your missus think about you being away so much?' I thought that would sort it.

Ah' He smiled. 'Not a pretty story, that.'

I decided to have the roast dinner 'cos I could never afford to cook a roast at home.

'She buggered off after thirteen months.' Alan looked me straight in the eye. 'Said she felt like a war widow and she divorced me in under two years. Not exactly the fastest divorce on record, but getting that way.'

'Haven't you bothered since?' Hope there's not a girlfriend gunna pull me hair out.'

'Oh Trace. What sort of life have you been living?'

'You don't want to know,' I muttered and pretended to be choosing from the menu. The waiter brought a rum and coke for me and another beer for Alan. Lily looked as proud as punch with her orange juice and lemonade which had ice and a straw in it.

'Can I have another if I want?'

'Ssh. Watch yer manners.' I noticed Alan was still smiling.

The dinner was fantastic. I had roast beef, the same as Alan, and Lily ordered sausage and chips. She asked the waitress if they had tomato sauce and grinned when they put a bottle on the table and left it within her reach. 'I'll put the sauce on,' I told her. I was imagining it going everywhere.

So...he wasn't married, he liked kids and he didn't seem to have heard any tittle tattle about me. So far so good, I thought. But I knew it would end in tears, cos that's how my life was. But I decided I might as well enjoy it while I could. And I was gonna have a pudding, too.

Mummy...there's one thing I keep thinking about...I'm not sure how to say it but...I wonder, if you and Daddy hadn't adopted me, would I have grown up in a family like Alfie's? Do you think...perhaps...I belong with Alfie...that he's more my sort of boy?

Lottie

The trial was drawing to a conclusion but we were still living with the nightmare of our precious daughter's coma. I was convinced Alfie Collins was going to prison and I couldn't wait for it to be over.

We tried to get life onto an even keel and I visited Saskia each afternoon with Mum when Tom was in court. One morning, when I had my head in the airing cupboard sorting the abundance of linen, I heard the phone ring. I knew Enid was around, but she hadn't heard it and Mum never answered the phone. I eventually caught the insistent ring.

'Lottie? Is that Lottie?'

My throat was dry and I coughed before answering. 'It is. Hello.' I knew it was Mark Erdington. He had a distinctive voice and when you'd imagined that call for as long as we had, the shock was palpable. Is Saskia dead? Are they going to switch off her life support? My mind was already in over-drive but I verbalised none of my jumbled thoughts, I just listened for the news that would surely impact on the rest of our lives.

'Hello Lottie. I'd like you and Tom to come in. If you can come right away, so much the better, but I could see you this afternoon, too.'

I didn't make a sound. The hideousness of the situation rendered me devoid of speech.

'We believe Saskia is in the first stages of waking... Lottie are you still there?... Her vital signs suggest a level of consciousness we've not seen and she's opened her eyes a couple of times. Can you get here fairly soon?'

The deluge of tears shouldn't have surprised me but they were so deep-seated and fierce that I thought they might choke me. 'Of course...of course. I'm sorry... I'm such a mess, and... I was expecting the worst.'

'Is Tom at home?'

'He's in court but I'll text him and we'll be straight there. Thanks. Thank you for calling. We'll see you soon.'

Enid appeared from somewhere and took the phone from my hand. 'Shall I contact Mr Hanson?'

'No, it's OK Enid. I'll text him and pick him up at the court...'

Tom insisted on driving so Mum and I made the journey to the hospital in silence. I did some deep breathing and convinced myself I would handle the next few hours with dignity, no matter what the outcome.

'It's funny,' Tom said as I stared at the road like a robot. 'You wait and wait and then when it happens you feel like a fish out of water. Do you feel like that too, Snooks?'

I had no idea how I felt other than scared witless and pleased Tom was by my side. Mum, bless her had nothing to say but was probably mirroring my feelings. I felt a ray of hope, not very bright; it was one long diminished by the enemy called fear. I was determined to stay strong and the time for tears was over. I prayed I could live up to my resolve and push aside all negative thoughts although it wasn't easy.

'It looks hopeful Snooks. But we mustn't get carried away. Small steps I think, that's what's needed. Who rang? His secretary'

'No, Mark rang. He wanted to give us the news himself. She's showing signs of coming out of the coma although she still wasn't conscious when he rang. They obviously expect her to come round, from the way he was talking.'

135

After months of waiting for news, I was petrified. Words stumbled around my mouth and I expected my legs to let me down. But it was time to buck up and stop persecuting myself about the state of Saskia's brain function. Who knew if my daughter would survive her ordeal intact? Only time would reveal that.

I didn't feel the tears run down my face in the car until a splash of water landed on my hand. Tom passed me an Enid-bright cotton hanky and I mopped myself up. Mum started a nervous chirp about God knows what from the back seat.

'It sounds hopeful love. They wouldn't have rung else. Would they?' She needed to fill the silence.

Actually they would. The call made no reference to a positive outcome. It was just what it said on the tin. Saskia had decided to wake and her mental state hung in the balance.

As usual it was difficult to park, but on a day when it really mattered we had a stroke of luck. Tom spotted a lady struggling to get her car out of a space and we waited patiently for her to move. Tom executed his precision parking between the white lines while Mum fumbled in her bag for parking money. We paid for three hours and decided we could feed the meter later, if needed.

Inside the hospital Mum wanted to go to the loo so we took a detour to accommodate her. Tom and I were on tender hooks as we stood in a cream-painted corridor, waiting for her to emerge from the hospital lavatories. We took a lift to Saskia's floor where Sister greeted us.

'Fingers crossed. We've all got everything crossed for you.' I gave her something I hoped resembled a smile.

Our favourite Thai nurse was preparing the drug trolley and she wished us luck, too. If good wishes represented a positive outcome, we were going to be OK. And then I thought about Michael Schumacher. I knew he'd been in a coma for years, so at least we were luckier than him. But was it all about degrees of luck? I felt it was. A roll of the dice could be the difference between having our beautiful daughter intact or... I refused to go there again, especially when we were entering the most positive phase of our daughter's coma.

I sat Mum on a chair outside Saskia's room. She held my hand and I could see she, too, was close to tears. It was the fear I remember most about that day, not relief or joy, we just shared the fear in our eyes. I was unsure what we would find in Saskia's room so felt it was safer to leave Mum outside on a visitor's chair.

We entered to find the room full of medics and it was uncomfortably hot. Everything was beeping as usual and I longed to open a window. Saskia's consultant caught our eye and indicated for us to return the way we'd come. Clearly Mark wanted to speak to us. He shook our hands as if it was a Rotary meeting and my mind was tumbling over itself for information.

'It is all looking good so far, but we have a way to go.'

Mark Erdington appeared calm but I guessed he, too, was anxious. 'Saskia gave eye contact to a nurse this morning and responded to a squeeze of her hand. I believe she's on her way but it will be slow.'

I longed for a bottle of water.

'She'll come up through various levels of consciousness and it could take some time. Hopefully, each stage will bring her closer to us.'

'What's your best guess, Mark?' It seemed the only question that mattered.

'I can only give a ball park estimate Lottie. I know this is excruciating for you both. This is never an exact science but I would expect her to be fully awake this evening, if all goes well.'

And if it doesn't? Did I say that out loud? No one answered so I guessed I hadn't. Mark disappeared.

I sat down next to Mum who grabbed my hand and kissed it. 'Oh Lottie. Can you believe this? Is this really happening?' She was shaking and her voice was weak. I squeezed her hand and told her we mustn't get ahead of ourselves. I'd lapsed into medical speak.

'Why don't you go in and say hello to Saskia? Tell her you're here.'

I turned to meet the eyes of a young doctor with an earnest look which would stand him in good stead when he made professor. His demeanour suggested he'd look the same in twenty years' time as he'd looked at thirteen.

'I think I'll stay here love. You know where I am if you need me.' Mum sat down with purpose.

Tom and I entered Saskia's room with so much hope it was a physical pain. She looked exactly the same as usual, cool and beautiful, but who could see degrees of consciousness? We didn't want to get in the way of the medical staff but they offered us seats either side of our daughter.

'Talk to her Mrs Hanson. Like you usually do. Anything is worth trying to bring her up.'

So we did. We kept it low-key, almost a whisper, but I told her how lovely the gardens were looking at home and I told her Justin Beiber was doing a concert in London soon. Tom said that he'd noticed Harrods had a sale on and he'd take her, if she woke up.

After three cups of tea on the ward and a quick trip to the hospital café, it was already seven o'clock. Tom had managed a cream tea while Mum and I toyed with Rich Tea biscuits and we heard on the TV news that Trump was the new President of the USA. I realised we didn't have a monopoly on problems. His grinning face poked from the television in the corner of the café and distracted us for a few minutes. When we returned to Saskia's room we were told 'things were on schedule,' but still she hadn't woken.

After another half hour of corridor sitting, while doctors carried out a procedure we weren't privy to, we were called to her bedside. Saskia was awake! She had her eyes open and there was definitely life in them. I noticed the silence in her room and realised the life-support machine no longer beeped and my daughter was breathing unaided. I held her hand, unable to hold back the tears. Even Tom looked remarkably close to breaking down.

'Mum....'

The medical students and doctors left the room to give us privacy and the nurses were as discreet as they could be. 'Ssh. You're better now darling. Daddy is here too. Don't try to talk just yet.'

A nurse gave her oxygen. 'She's a good colour. You look rosy pink Saskia. Quite beautiful in fact.'

I blessed her for the comment. Nothing would please our daughter more than being told she looked beautiful.

Tom reached for Saskia's other hand and we gazed at our daughter in disbelief. She really was awake and talking to us. Did that mean there was no brain damage? I couldn't even form the question.

We sat with her a while and then I suggested to Tom that Mum would like to see her. It was an emotional moment. We'd all dreamed of it happening and yet it was incredibly hard to deal with. Half of me was sighing with relief and the rest of me was weeping with dread. Staff Nurse explained Saskia would undergo various tests and it could take a couple of days for all the results to come in. So more waiting. I was resigned to waiting and nothing could spoil that precious moment. Saskia would sleep for many hours over the coming days, the nurses informed us.

'Granny, thanks for being here.'

Mum cried unfettered tears. It was hard for us to process the moment. In my usual analytical way I was encouraged that Saskia recognised Mum and put it in my bag of positives which was heavier than it had been for weeks.

We didn't want to leave but the nurses eventually persuaded us to go home; it was a squeak after eleven o'clock and Mum was nearly asleep on her feet.

'Saskia isn't going anywhere,' the Houseman joked. 'She'll still be here in the morning and nurses will sit with her all night. She's likely to sleep until morning. Come back after you've had some rest and you'll be ready to face tomorrow.'

He looked about sixteen and I envied him his confidence. I had so many questions and as yet, there were no answers. Would staying all night by her side have prevented something terrible happening? No, it wouldn't. Had we got a long-haul ahead of us to get Saskia fully recuperated? Yes we had.

And so I followed my own advice. Tom looked relieved and then I remembered he was in court the following day. I knew for certain I wouldn't be in the public gallery beside him; Saskia would come above bloody Alfie Collin's trial, of that I was sure.

We drove the dark, quiet streets in silence, yet I felt we should be celebrating. I craved a gin and tonic and it needed to be light on the tonic; I knew Tom would need at least two fingers of malt. Mum just wanted her bed.

Tom threw the house into a blaze of yellow light which made us squint. He unlocked the front door and placed the keys on the hall table before he fell into my arms. I rocked his body into mine while he sobbed into my shoulder.

'Oh Snooks. I thought she was gone for ever. I never thought she'd open her eyes again.'

Mum indicated she was going to bed and disappeared upstairs.

I was staggered by Tom's outpouring. He'd never indicated his distress throughout our ordeal and behind all that outer show of coping, he was a broken man. I held him tight and tried to calm his heaving shoulders. I tried to melt love through our bodies and found I was crying too. This time it was for Tom. I cried for my selfishness in blocking him out and found it cathartic. Crying for someone you love is cleansing and somehow it took away the angst and emotion of the last few days. We had our daughter back and that was the most important thing. Any complications and all the 'what ifs,' they were for another day.

Tracey

They did something called the summing up and the case
was close to being over. I decided to get to court early 'cos
I'd spotted a place where it would be easy for Alfie to see
me. I wanted to give him a smile when they took him down.
I wanted him to know I was going to do everything I could
to get him out. I'd have done anything to see him walk
through our door again.

It didn't sound like there was a cat's chance in hell that
he'd get off, but at least he'd know I'd been there for him
every day. That stuffed shirt from the college told the court
that Alfie was given *an opportunity boys like him would
give their right arm for'*. Then he told everybody how my
Alfie *'squandered what he was given*. He said my boy
'threw it back in our faces.' I wanted to put a cowpat in his
bleeding face. That's what I'd have liked to do.

I'd heard on the local jungle drums that Alfie might have
been set up. Nothing stayed a secret where we lived. It
sounded like another bloke was involved with knifing the
girl, but nothing came out in court. In a way, that made it
worse 'cos how can it be cut and dried if there's doubt
about who did it? Alfie told me from the beginning he
never done it. He told me there was another bloke involved
but....shit....I never believed my own boy. What sort of
mother did that make me? I continued to zone in and out of
the technical talk which mostly went over me head. I just
wanted them to announce the bottom line.

Suddenly it was over. The days and days putting my Alfie
down was over. I hoped those posh gits from the college
were happy, seeing my lad go down for six years. I stood
with everybody else when the snooty cow of a judge left,
but I wasn't sure me legs would carry me out.

I leaned against the stone pillar in the court lobby and
tried to work out if I could reach a seat that was only a few
feet away. If my knees gave way I'd have ended up making
a spectacle of meself. Deep down, I never really expected

141

Alfie to come home, but I kidded myself something magical would come along and get him off.

My friend Charlene offered to come for the verdict, but I knew she'd lose money if she took time off from the factory. So I lied. I said mother was coming to court with me. Now I was on me own, fighting nausea and tears and that wasn't my way, was it? I'd never been a wimp.

I was still gathering courage to reach the seat when the defence brief made me jump out of me skin. I've always hated it when people creep up on me.

'I'm sorry Ms Collins, I thought we had a slim chance, but it wasn't to be.'

I thought for one awful moment he was going to put his arm around me. I sidled towards the seat. Four paces, I prayed I'd make four paces. I glared at the stuck-up prick.

'Still, never mind eh? You still get paid, don't you?

'I wouldn't say that has any relevance, Ms Collins. I'm sincerely sorry Alfie was

sentenced. But we always knew it was likely, didn't we?

'We did, did we?' He didn't even speak like a normal person. 'Well you might have been bleeding well expecting it, but I wasn't. 'It was your job to get him off.' I caught an adrenaline burst and stomped towards the door. All I wanted was to go home.

As I reached the wide stone steps of the courthouse, all hell let loose. Cameras and microphones were pushed into me face, flashlights popped and everyone was shouting.

'Have you been to see Saskia Hanson?'

'How does it feel to know your son tried to murder a young girl?'

'Did you know Alfie took drugs?'

I looked around in desperation. My hand leapt unaided to me mouth and me eyes

skittered like a frightened rabbit.

'This way. Come this way.' A man elbowed his way through the crowd towards me. I had no idea who the broad, beefy fellow was, but I followed him anyway.

'Stand aside. Let the lady though.'

'She ain't no lady,' called a wag in the crowd. 'I'm sure I put a paper bag on her head

last week.'

There was a titter of appreciation for the humour. Next I found myself shoehorned into a car with its engine idling. Bulbs flashed off the windscreen and there were shouts of rage that I'd slipped the net. I knew the maggot reporters got some pictures, but I didn't care. The car lurched down Rosalind Street and took a side turning into Aldrich Way. About half way down the driver signalled he was pulling over and he shot into a parking space.

'Who the bleeding hell are you? I spat at him like shale on a beach.

'I'm probably your saving grace and a thank you wouldn't go amiss.'

'Never asked you to pick me up.'

'What did you think was going to happen to you? Nice cosy chat with the reporters

over a cup of tea?'

I looked at him and for the first time noticed he'd got a taxi driver's licence stuck to his dashboard. 'Listen love. You're not the first mother to see her son go down and you won't be the last. Only difference is, they usually have a few family or friends with them. Bit of a Billy-No-Mates, are you?'

'Don't need nobody. I can manage on me own. And don't think you'll get a quick blow-job out of this, 'cos you won't.'

He looked at me like I'd shocked him with my blunt-speaking. He was plump with a grey beard and not much hair and was probably old enough to be my grandfather. 'Listen love. The whole world's not your enemy.'

'It bleeding well is from where I'm standing.'

'Well today it's not. OK? Now, where to? It's on me.'

He dropped me at me flat and true to his word, it was a free ride with no strings. I was glad to be home and had half an hour to meself before I needed to collect Lily from school. I put the kettle on and sank into the sofa while it boiled and texted Mum to tell her not to bother to fetch Lily. I told her about Alfie, too. What the hell would become of my Alfie? He'd messed his life up bigtime and it was my fault. He had a lousy mother.

I'd seen that girl's parents in court. The mother looked pale and close to tears most of the time and her wanker of a father just looked straight ahead when he was in the dock; like he had a smell under his nose. Stuck-up pricks, both of them.

I was still asking myself if Alfie gave that girl drugs? Did he leave her to die? After everything I'd heard in court, I still didn't have an answer. I didn't want to think the worst of him. Of course I didn't. But it was hard to argue when his finger prints were on the knife.

I could remember Alfie came home that night. It was his birthday and he came in late, I heard him thumping about in his bedroom and I worried he'd wake Lily. But had he just knifed a young girl? The law said he did. But what was that girl doing with him, I wanted to know? Mum told me no good would come of my Alfie using the art school at the college. 'He'll not fit in,' she'd said. Clearly she was wrong, as usual. He seemed to have fitted in a treat.

I've never done anything so exciting as being with Alfie. He's sexy Mummy. Really sexy. Even better than Oli Mures. But you don't need to worry about me... We took everything at a slow pace. Honestly... I told him I was a virgin... but then he touched me where no one has ever touched me, he kissed me and searched until I allowed his tongue into my mouth; he sent tingles to the very core of me, Mummy. I couldn't help myself. He wants to marry me. I know he's not like one of us but he'll fit in. Eventually. When you get to know him you'll like him.

I started to believe Saskia was functioning fully after her miraculous awakening. The effect was biblical in proportion.

The Way It Is

On the third day I found her sitting up in bed and her nurse said she could venture into a chair that afternoon. Small steps, but they were enough to make my heart sing. She was still on a drip; the staff wanted to be sure her swallow reflex was reliable before allowing her solid food. And she was alert, although we'd been asked not to talk about the events leading to her coma. That was the difficult bit.

The registrar told us, 'There will be plenty of time for details later. And she may not remember anything about her ordeal. We prefer any kind of interaction to be done by people who are trained in these things. Try to keep conversations short and light-hearted.' He also informed us the police were waiting to interview her but they wouldn't be given access for a few days, at the earliest. We had no choice but to follow instruction but news about the police interview gave me something else to worry about in the middle of the night.

Poor Tom sat in court for the final few days while Mum and I spent every waking hour with Saskia. He found it stressful and struggled to communicate about the day's proceedings when he came back from his gruelling days. Of course, I was anxious to hear of any progress but Tom was zapped out with the trauma of it. Giving evidence was tolerable, he told me, but hearing intimate details about the event made him feel sick. Of course, Saskia had no idea what was happening and it needed to stay that way, until she was fully recovered.

Each day I noticed small improvements. She had physiotherapy twice a day to begin with but her body was so weak she was unable to support her own weight. She was a shadow of our feisty daughter but we felt blessed that we had her back.

And so, it was Tom who brought Mum and I the good news that Alfie Collins was going to prison for six years. I knew it could be reduced for good behaviour, but that did nothing to spoil the joy we felt that justice for our daughter had been done.

145

Tom and I took Mum home to Cirencester where she had
a warm welcome from Dad who'd missed her cooking.

'Nobody does a roast like your mother,' he said.

He was preaching to the converted. Mum started tutting
about the layers of dust over the furniture and I reminded
her of Dad's age and that running the farm was already a
full time job.

*Alfie isn't like Dad's boys. He isn't...well educated. He talks
tough and he can be mean. But he's sooo cool. He even
smells exciting. He wears this great aftershave that melts
me every time he's near... My head still feels messed up. I
had vodka Mum – a lot of vodka. Don't be cross with me.
And Alfie tried to rescue me. He thumped a man who was
hurting me and they both fell on top of me. I felt a really bad
pain in my stomach...it was so bad. They were fighting on
top of me and then...they rolled onto the floor. I saw the
knife sticking out of my tummy but I felt so fuzzy I had no
idea what to do.... I think I...love him Mum.*

I was pretty sure when my daughter woke she'd want
nothing more to do with that lad. Especially when she knew
he'd been sent to prison. Surely she'd see all of his...
inadequacies. And she would carry the scars from the knife
for the rest of her life. It must have been a mad moment,
probably just the thrill of something different. I was looking
for answers and part of me toyed with the nurture/nature
conundrum. Were her instincts more nature than nurture?
Were her birth-mother's drug and sexual issues somewhere
deep in Saskia's DNA? We might never have an answer to
that.

They talked about Saskia going home after ten days of
consciousness, provided she kept all the physiotherapy
appointment and continued her counselling sessions. She'd
managed her first shower with support from me and I'd
washed her hair in the streaming water. But she was
exhausted from the effort it required and slept for most of

that day. I woke her to eat but she pecked like a bird at everything I tried to tempt her with.

Tracey

I hadn't noticed but I'd started crying and it caught me off-guard 'cos I never cried. Well not very often. But how could my Alfie bear it? Locked up with no hope? I had to do something. I was slumped on the sofa feeling totally useless. It was enough to make me get the Christmas sherry out but I had to fetch Lily from school.

There was a small ray of hope though. Dickie told Mum he reckoned he could get Alfie off. Said he'd find someone to put up an alibi for him. But I knew he was all talk. You always got a lot of swanky talk from him, but...I couldn't help wondering - what if for once, he was right.

And then, like a bad smell the old man let himself in through my front door. He'd got fat by then and he rolled his body into the arm chair, letting out a groan like he was in pain. I couldn't hide a look of disgust.

'Been crying, girl?'

'No. I've got a bit of hay fever is all.'

'Going to see the lad?'

'Yeh. Corse.'

'Not good in there, Trace. Lot of trouble on the wings.'

'Like you'd know.'

'I know alright. I'm in the know about all sorts of things you don't know about.'

I'd heard about the theft and beatings in prisons. Everybody knew about that. I could hardly bear to think about my Alfie getting hurt.

'Pretty Boy' that's what the bastards are calling Alfie. I heard he's getting a lot of stick 'cos of his looks.'

I was dumbstruck for a minute or two. Couldn't think what to say.

'I heard he might get his head shaved. Thinks it'll make him look tougher. Sometimes the perverts wait 'til the youngsters 'aint looking and then make a grab fer them in the shower.'

'Shit. You're lying. How the hell would you know?'

'As long as he's got money, he won't get into too much trouble, Trace.'

'What sort of trouble?' I searched Dickie's eyes for signs that he was lying. I'd had plenty of experience of that.

'Don't know as I should tell you really. Me neighbour's nephew, Greggo Hewitt, is on the same wing and he has lots to say about the goings on.'

'And?'

'You sure you want to know? Don't whinge to me if you don't like it.'

'Corse I wanna know. What'd you take me for? A wuss?'

'OK. Well.....' Dickie took time to blow his nose. Snuffled and snorted like a hedgehog after milk. 'There's a nonce on the wing who likes young, dark kids. Big bugger. Says he's got a passion for black haired youngsters. Likes your Alfie's skin, he said.'

'What! You gotta be kidding me. Alfie ain't no nonce.'

'Never said he was. This bloke just takes what he fancies. Screws turn a blind eye, so I've heard.'

I had to sit down. Alfie was a lot of things, but he wasn't a nonce. He'd had more women than I'd had hot dinners.

'I can help fix it, you know.' I recognised the whining voice and his eyes told me there was a catch.

'Oh yeh. And how can you keep my Alfie safe? Going in for a stretch yerself are yer?'

'Not me. But Greggo Hewitt's already in there, like I said and he's prepared to make a little deal with you.'

'Why me? What's he want with me?' I could feel it wasn't going well.

'There's lots you can do for a man on the inside - especially if you're prepared to do a favour for the right people. See what I mean?

I kinda did but it was thin on details and I didn't like what I was hearing. Dickie went to put the kettle on, just like the old days. Thought he still owned me but a lot had happened since those days.

'There you go me little Pidgeon Pie.' He put two mugs of tea on the table. I grabbed the mug and clasped me fingers round it. It was too hot to drink but I didn't want him shovelling sugar in it.

'Spit it out then. Might as well cut to the chase.'

'Not so hasty. You always were hasty. Sometimes you've gotta just mull thing over a bit. See how it fits.'

'So how exactly does it *fit*?'

'I'm just thinking how this could work. Best fer everybody. You know?

I hadn't got a fuckin' clue what he was talking about. 'Best fer you, yer mean?'

'I could be hurt by that remark if I didn't know you. Luckily, I know yer don't mean it. Always spouting yer mouth off, ain't you?'

I couldn't argue with that. Mum always says I'd got a mouth like a barn door.

'I still don't get it. Talk straight, will you?'

Dickie took a slurp of tea. I was sick to my stomach about what was coming'. He added another spoonful of sugar to his mug. Made me wait.

'OK. ....OK.......You can't wait fer nothing can yer? It's like this. Greggo's got a little business running outside what's going to waste. He said he'll keep an eye on Alfie, if you get me drift, and you can do a bit of business for him.

OMG. I just knew he wanted me back on the game. But I could imagine Alfie being hurt. 'What sort of business?' I already knew I was done for.

'Well here's the thing. Ever heard of SPICE?'

I shook me head. 'Old Spice. Like you used to wear? He must have thought I was stupid.'

Dickie chuckled. Nasty, mean sort of chuckle it was. 'You crease me up Trace. Ain't lost yer sense of humour have you? No. This is a drug. Synthetic it is – made in back rooms. You know?'

149

Actually I didn't know and I didn't want to.

'Best currency there is in jail. But the best bit is, they haven't got a test for it yet and sniffer-dogs can't get a handle on it, neither. They pull inmates in for drug tests but they can't detect SPICE. The perfect drug I'd call it. Prisons are rife with it, right across the country.

'I aint peddling no drugs. I've got my Lily to think about. Who'd look after her if I'm inside? Me mother? I don't think so.'

'No...... yer not getting it.'

'That's 'cos you ain't telling it straight Dickie.'

'OK. This is the thing. SPICE is passing round in prison like a whore's panties. Never seen it meself but they call it a 'legal high'. Not legal in her Majesty's prisons, though, is it?' He's looking at me like I'm daft. Like I don't know about drugs. 'But it's got to be paid for, of course. Know how they do that?

I hadn't got a clue, but I soon would.

'They take the money off the little woman indoors. Her at home with the kids. That's how.' He was still digging his nose out and wiping green bogies on his hanky and it was beginning to make me feel sick

In about half an hour, after two cups of tea and much wheedling, I had the lot. The men take the SPICE and the wives pay their bills. The deal on the table was that I set up a credit round, collecting money each week from the families of the prisoners. I'd have me own driver. Apparently, they liked to have a woman call for the money 'cos it didn't look as suspicious as a bloke. The old bastard even suggested I take Lily with me. Like hell I would. He thought it would be a good cover. Yeh, right. I'd be sure to do that. He reckoned the Old Bill got wise to the game after a time so I'd have to go careful. Too right I would. I said I'd think about it and Dickie said, 'don't think too long 'cos you never know who might be stretching Alfie a bit.' OMG. Did he mean what I thought he meant?

I had to get tea for Lily. She kept talking about Alfie 'cos kids at school had teased her about her brother being in prison. It was hard. Who wants their daughter to know that kinda stuff? While they held him in custody, waiting for the trial, I told her he'd gone travelling. Africa. It was the first thing that came into me head. Now she knew the truth and it didn't make her life easy.

I'd read in the paper about that poor girl. The girl at his party. I still couldn't get my head round my Alfie doing that to her. Drugs maybe. He might have given her drugs. But knifing her? Never.

The court said Alfie's finger prints were on the knife and there were witnesses who seen her at his party. His DNA was all over her, they said. I was in shock. Then the ditzy woman what arranged for him to paint at Churchill's College stood up in court and said he was a good boy. She said she'd never seen Alfie with a knife. She didn't think he could have done it. But they didn't believe her did they? I 'spose it was all my fault. I let him get away when he was a kid. Never kept tabs on what he was up to.

Old Dickie knows I'll do it. He knows I'm soft about me kids.

Crime and Retribution?

Watery sunshine washes the concrete high-rise, highlighting the vision some middle class wanker had for the masses, years before. A fag-end flirts with a crisp packet on the breeze and a bike is rusting on a patch of crappy grass. 'Skankland,' as the living block is quaintly known, is at the rougher end of rough.

Alfie swaggers to the second floor and takes the disintegrating concrete steps two at a time. Designer jeans hang low over narrow hips and his leather jacket would laugh in the face of Matalan. An wrap-around black scarf masks his face and wisps of dark hair escape and catch the breeze. Nothing vaguely athletic has ever bothered his baseball boots.

He eyeballs the row of doors, on high alert for cameras and snoopers. A Christmas streamer tangles with a dustbin lid. Satisfied he has no on-lookers, he turns the key on number thirty two and slips inside.

There's no word of greeting from the old man who's glued to the forty inch colour monitor. The curtains haven't been drawn back for days and the accumulated gloom is thick as bread pudding. Alfie makes a mental note of cigarette butts spilling from the old man's ashtray and quietly places a Yale key on the sideboard. Unnoticed, he removes the telephone from the old man's reach.

There's a whiff of decay and poverty has marked both the man and his possessions.

'Yer up then?'

'Corse I am. It's nearly bloody dinnertime.'

Alfie's nose wrinkles at the stench of pee emanating from a tube that drips urine into a glass jar at Dickie's feet. It's the colour of orange juice.

Meagre heat seeps from an electric fire which accounts for the old man's muffled appearance; his hunkered torso is fattened by layers of clothing which make a robust man of him. Mucous gathers like stalactites on elongated nose hair and his fingers worry a stained blanket wrapped around his lower limbs. He wears a chunky rib-knit cardigan, wrongly buttoned and splattered with yesterday's dinner. A grey shirt is visible around his scrawny neck and a knitted hat sits low over rheumy eyes. A metal Manchester United badge is pinned upside down into the red, loose-knitted wool.

'I delivered that bit of paperwork you gave me.' Alfie runs his finger through layers of dust on a small table. 'Snotty blonde tart in the office asked who I was. I told her to mind her own. Jumped up cow.'

'Spose yer good for something, then. Did yer steam it open? Have a look did yer?'

'As if.'

The old man's smoking. A gnarled hand peppered with age spots flicks ash somewhere handy to the ashtray. He's a fifty fags a day bloke with a cough to prove it. Nobody suggests he should give them up and he wouldn't give a damn if they did.

Alfie crosses to the window and swishes the curtains back against the wall, allowing new light to lift the gloom.

'Heh, what yer doing?' The old man's arms spasm objection. 'I like it dark. Draw them curtains back.'

A solitary tree crowds through the pane and skitters sunlight across the old man's face, ghosting his skin. Alfie opens the window. Wide.

'Shut that fuckin' window. I'm froze to the marrow here.'

'Shut it yerself Old Man.' Alfie ambles back. Puts himself in the old man's face and catches the stench of decay. 'Oh I forgot. You can't, can yer 'cos yer legs don't work. Ha. Not such a big man these days, are you?'

The old man mutters about yobs with fuckin' earrings who think they know it all. He gives an exaggerated shiver and hugs himself.

'I'm froze. What yer playing at?'

'It needs some fresh air in here Old Man.'

'Need some fuckin' money to pay the lecki bill. Yer letting all the fuckin'

heat out.'

'I told you I'd sort it. Yer bill. 'Has it come in?'

'Don't need charity.'

A commode, courtesy of the Red Cross, is coyly covered with a lace tray cloth next to a pile of clothes. The utilitarian sideboard, brown and screaming for polish, is devoid of family photos, china dogs or a clock. There's a well-used whisky bottle and a dirty glass lingering on a small table.

The old man lights the umpteenth fag of the day and turns up the volume on the television. He ignores his visitor who's sizing-up the room with the nose of an estate agent. 'Loose Women' add glamour and volume to the late morning.

'Cut it out Old Man. I've come to visit haven't I?' Alfie takes command of the remote control. 'Can't hear meself think with them stupid bitches rattling on.'

The old man scowls. 'My tele'.

'Is that your idea of a bit of totty these days?' Alfie gives a scathing snort. 'At least yer leaving me Mum alone, I 'spose.'

The old man's tremor causes the cigarette to dance in his hand. His eyes leak rheumy drips. 'Nobody asked you to fuckin' come.'

'Nice. Very nice. Nobody asks for a lot of things, Old Man. Don't mean they won't get them.' Alfie scrutinises the room with darting, toffee eyes.

'Fuckin' riddles. All you ever talk is fuckin' riddles. Why don't you piss off and leave me in peace?'

'It's Christmas. Want any groceries Old Man?'

'Don't want nothing and Christmas don't matter to me. Same as any other day of the year.'

'Please yerself'.

'At least I can still do that.'

Alfie helps himself to one of the old man's cigarettes and lights it with an exaggerated inhalation. He holds the smoke in his respiratory track, revisiting the joy of that first drag after months of abstinence in prison. He blows smoke rings in the old man's face which heralds a phlegmy cough. 'Better get that cough seen to. Might carry yer off, one of these days.'

'Where's yer manners?'

'My manners left years ago. 'Round about the time you crawled into me Mum's bed. Got you to thank fer having no manners.'

Alfie makes a casual inspection of the old man's medical notes sitting in a blue folder which are used by the plethora of helpers who keep his life afloat. 'On the Social now? Nice. Where's yer money gone, Old Man?

'None of yer business.'

'Oh yes, I forgot. You lost it all. Just like you lost yer legs. Very careless letting yobs beat you up in the alley.'

'Shut yer trap. I do alright. And anyway, buy your own bleeding fags. They cost a fortune these days.'

A pack of cigarettes appears on the arm of the chair. 'There you go. Don't say I never give you anything.' Alfie smirks at the pathetic old man.

'Don't smoke them sort. Time you knew what I smoke.' He picks them up and squirrels them under the duvet.

'Thought I'd keep you company Old Man. What with it being Christmas. Got a turkey have you? I 'spect even an ungrateful shit like you likes a bit of turkey.' Alfie sits himself down on an orange plastic pouffe and faces the breathing bag of bones. 'This is comfy.' He wriggles around to settle his backside.

'That's for me feet, kid.' The old man flaps his arms in protest.

'Cantankerous ain't you? I'll not nick it you know.' Alfie arranges his long legs around the circumference of the pouffe. 'Comfy.'

'Never mind about comfy. Shut that bleeding window. The sun makes me squint and it's like Siberia in here.'

'Quit carping. You'll soon be nice and toasty Old Man. Very soon'

'More bloody riddles. Clear off.'

'I'm going. But you, if I was you, I'd have a nice long sleep.'

Alfie places his glowing cigarette into the surface of the orange stool, waits until it melts the plastic, smiles and leaves the old man to warm up.

Rita Trotman

Five Years Later - Christmas 2017

Lottie

I've been watching Tom argue with a bouncing Labrador that's infringed our garden boundary. The dog wanted to play but had no chance of a ball game with Tom, so it disappeared, leaving its slobbered-on ball to linger on the grass. It made me smile and has me day-dreaming. Life is good again and the trauma of our daughter's near-death experience is fading like a bad smell, although it's never quite forgotten because you pick at the scars when least expected. But we are slowly managing to leave it where it belongs, which is in the past.

The winter pansies need planting-up in the pots outside the kitchen window but I'm making chutney, so they'll have to wait. The glut of tomatoes arrived on the kitchen table this morning, curtesy of the gardener who cheerily boasted he'd, 'stripped the glasshouse bare.' The aroma has passed from yummy to throat-numbing and will probably linger for days. Olivia is 'helping' which has slowed me down, but I love having my granddaughter around. She's nothing like Saskia was as a child; mostly she listens to what I tell her and she has a calmer approach to life. At the moment, she's covered in tomato juice and looks totally adorable.

It was a tricky time before Olivia's birth. Life was filled to capacity with more than baby issues as we both embraced having Saskia home. There was freshness to each morning and hope returned to spur us on to help our daughter return to full health. I searched for the old Saskia in the shadow of the new one, but some days the view was misted. It was a slow process, but at least we had something to encourage and sustain us daily.

Saskia was in a stubborn mood when she first woke from her coma. However, our concerns about her brain function quickly dispersed as her intellect proved sharper than a Stanley knife. Sometimes I joked with Tom that a long sleep had made her what Dad would call 'mardy.' Nothing we did pleased her and anything suggested to ease her through the last trimester of her pregnancy, was met with resistance. No matter how we coaxed or cajoled, some days she barely rose from her bed, although I drew the line at room service. Enid was banned from fetching and carrying for her, too. Tom was able to appease her moods more readily than me and I waited expectantly for the return of my witty, charming daughter.

In the early weeks she was less than a ray of sunshine around the house but Mark Erdington assured us this was normal after her experiences. And so we danced to her tune, always mindful of how close we came to losing her.

When Saskia eventually acknowledged her pregnancy, (having initially told me I was talking nonsense,) she seesawed between keeping her baby and giving it up for adoption. Although I tried to be supportive, if the adoption option became a reality, I had no idea how I would cope. Tom of course, was all for it. He felt his wishes had been ignored over the abortion issue and blatantly encouraged our daughter to give up her baby and get on with her life.

Saskia still hankered after a medical profession so she caught up with her exams at the local community college. She wasn't brave enough to continue at Churchill's, and who could blame her? But there was a part of me, the mischievous particle that remained of my previous self, that envisaged a pregnant Saskia at Churchill's. I suspected there'd have been a scattering of apoplectic figures at risk of heart failure. But we knew Saskia was bright enough to pick up her studies and had no concerns that she would make the cut for medical school. I admired her pluck; she was very obviously pregnant but showed no embarrassment among her fellow students.

Saskia and I bonded while we drove to pre-natal classes once a week and I glimpsed her old self beneath the grumpy moods and withdrawal from family life. I usually booked a table for dinner so that the classes became more of an occasion and I saw signs we were getting our loving daughter back. On occasion, she mentioned Alfie and I had to accept that if she kept the baby, he would be given access.

'I want her to know who her dad is. It's important. Being an adopted child, it's something I'll never know.'

It was gut-wrenching to know our daughter pined for something I couldn't give her and I worried it would blight her life. I talked to her about the possibility of Tom and me taking responsibility for the baby when it arrived. I told her we could keep it until she was ready to be a mother. I even suggested she might like a trip to Scilly after the baby was born, I thought some time apart would help her make the right decision about her child.

And then two milestones arrived at once. Our granddaughter made her entrance into the world and Tom gave his notice to Churchill's College. He'd decided, sadly without any reference to me that we would move to the family seat near Oxford. It appeared Tom felt unable to carry out his work at Churchill's after the court case and I could understand that. Given the opportunity, I'd have been a good listener.

When he looked for Headships in various parts of the country, I knew he was unsettled. I was bracing myself for a move, but moving to his inherited home was something I didn't see coming. By the time he shared his plans with me he'd already given his cousin notice and was making preparations for our new life. I was totally unprepared and it was nothing short of earth-shifting.

Meanwhile, we had to face the fact that Alfie Collins would have access to his daughter. Saskia would not be moved on the issue so we tried to accept it. Any argument we put forward was ignored. I tried to hide my irritation with my daughter and constantly reminded myself how close we'd come to losing her. But it wasn't easy. The sleepless nights continued and it seemed my head had no respite from worry even though the goal post had moved.

The Way It Is

When Alfie was released from prison he door-stepped the house for days. He'd heard Saskia was home and pregnant and eventually we had to let him see her. I insisted there would be no bedroom visits, so Saskia dressed and put on makeup before he was allowed in.

Tom had to deal with the logistics of Alfie's first visit, as it was beyond my ability to welcome that scoundrel into our home. But invade my private space he did and when he left, I felt violated; It was as if we'd had a burglar in our home. However, it became obvious he would not renege on his right to see his child, so eventually I managed to nod an acceptance when he was in my home.

While the weather stayed fine Saskia and Alfie sat in the garden, out of our earshot while they planned, who knew what? I was paranoid about his ability to influence my daughter and scared witless the relationship would linger. I think Tom worried who would see him on Churchill's soil. But over the weeks I noticed a gradual loss of interest from Saskia. A couple of times when Alfie came to see her she sent him away saying she was unwell. I revelled in those moments.

And Saskia's disinterest in Alfie was borne out one afternoon when we were shopping for baby clothes. Out of nowhere came the request I'd longed to hear, at last Saskia asked me to be her birthing partner. I'd been afraid the yob would welcome our grandchild into the world, but now the joy was going to be mine.

Luckily, after keeping me on tender hooks for days, Saskia agreed Tom and I could bring up her daughter while she got her life back on track. She showed no interest in Olivia from the moment she was born and Tom and I had to persuade her to name her baby daughter. Eventually I threatened to choose a name myself, which did the trick.

And so I took a wriggling Olivia Charlotte into my arms when she was born and we've loved her every day since her arrival. I did the night feeds and the nappy changing and I took her to clinic to be weighed and vaccinated. She felt as though she was mine although I was always mindful that she was on loan. Saskia took the odd look into the pram and was grumpy if woken at night by her crying infant.

The minefield that was Alfie Collins was ever present and impossible to eradicate and I could see he was in our lives for the long haul. But although I hated him near our granddaughter, the legal decision was not in my hands. I fully agreed the lad shouldn't linger in prison if, indeed, he hadn't wielded the knife nor pumped my daughter full of drugs, but I needed to distance him from our lives. Being a realist, I knew that wasn't to be.

And so the Hansons and the Collins families mingled over the crib. Alfie professed to love Saskia while she was more guarded about her feelings, although she cared enough to ensure all his convictions were dropped. The Appeal Hearing was gruelling. Prior to it happening, long hours were spent in the police station, many of them sitting in grubby corridors and many more under immense pressure as I watched Saskia handle the interrogation about the fateful night. When the police officer noted Saskia was pregnant she was asked if there was to be an allegation of rape. There wasn't. Eventually the law was satisfied that Alfie Collins was innocent of the crimes and agreed to his release.

'I like him Mummy but....he doesn't talk much and...we don't have much in common, I suppose.'

Except sex, I thought.

Tom had never mentioned any embarrassment over the problems we encountered with Saskia, although it was inevitable they had an impact on his life at Churchill's. I guess I was so wrapped up in my own worries that I didn't care about anything else. I had occasionally wondered if his job would survive, especially when the gruesome details about sex and drugs were made common knowledge at the trial, but it felt trivial compared to having a daughter in a drug fuelled coma.

With hindsight, I don't believe Tom was pushed from his position of House Master, but he probably felt alone while making major decisions about both his career and the wellbeing of his family. Which, I suppose makes me an insensitive bitch. But I paid the price because the move to the family seat got under way early in the Michaelmas term, whether I liked it or not.

'It will be a great place to bring up Olivia,' Tom persuaded me. 'And I'll make sure my mother doesn't interfere. I promise,' I was less than sure about that. Things moved quickly and before Olivia's first birthday, we were settled in the baronial home with the mother–in–law –from- hell ensconced in the Gatehouse on the edge of the estate.

Saying goodbye to Churchill's was harder than I expected, especially as we were inundated with gifts from all quarters. Boy's arrived at our apartment with sentimental cards and presents and the school gave us a stunning antique chest which we'll cherish. From the staff, we had a framed water colour of our house which encompasses the beautiful garden over which I'd pondered for so many hours while Saskia lay sleeping. I felt deeply humbled by the outpouring of love for our family and it only made it harder to move on with our lives.

My friend Heidi told me to 'buck up' when she found me in tears at the kitchen table the day before the move. She reminded me I was about to embark upon an exciting challenge and I was a 'lucky bunny' to be inheriting a Cotswold pile and a title. She practiced a curtsy and said she was damned if she was going to call me 'Ma'am. Of course she made me laugh and we made promises to stay in touch.

Dear Enid was another matter. She was unable to hide her dismay at our departure and at one point I thought Tom might offer her a cottage on the estate. But we left with our little family intact; I wallowed in the joy of having Saskia back and caring for her beautiful daughter.

When we tipped up at Knoxbury Hall I was still in aftershock from the unexpected changes to our lives. Olivia had just started walking so she was all over the place and certainly had no intention of being contained for more than an hour or two. Consequently, I had little input to the packing or unpacking of our belongings. It was a slightly surreal experience. We wanted to be in the Hall before Christmas and the whole operation was completed in less than a week. 'Put the crystal in the glass cabinet. No…the other glass cabinet.' I may not have made a physical contribution to the move, but my throat was raw from calling instructions. Our new home was already stuffed with antique furniture so we had to juxtaposition our own where we could. I had always thought our living space was generous at Churchill's, but this was gargantuan by comparison. Mum and Dad came up for a few hours to help, but we happily left the donkey work to the professionals. It was, however, lovely to have them share Olivia's boisterous energy.

Tom announced before we moved that he had plans to open the house to the public in order to pay for its upkeep. Around two hundred acres had been rented out by Tom's brother years before, but the income came nowhere near what was required. There was a herd of one hundred Devon Red cattle on the other hundred acres and an enclosure of angora sheep. Apparently, we were going to convert a barn into a tea room and make ice cream in the old dairy. We might find someone to spin the angora wool into saleable skeins, I offered. Tom had decided we'd employ local people to get his ideas off the ground and I was to have the luxury of part-time child care for Olivia. Things skipped along according to plan, mostly, and over the next few years the estate became more than self-sufficient

Tracey

I heard that girl woke up and I was as pleased for her family as anyone else. But the real shock came when my Alfie announced I was going to be a grandmother. He was like a dog with two tails but I could see beyond the first flush of excitement and I worried how it would work out. I didn't want him hurt, although he assured me his name was on the birth certificate.

What with the trauma of Alfie going down and the death of Old Dickie, I'd had a lot to deal with. When Dickie died, I wasn't sure how I felt, if I'm honest. It must have been a terrible death, being burnt alive and I wouldn't wish that on anyone. I don't think there was much of him left to put in a coffin. My Lily cried 'cos she liked the old sod. But me, it was a different matter for me 'cos he was answerable for a lot that was wrong with my life. But I eventually came to realise what he was, and I wouldn't be remembering him as a kind old man who took pity on a struggling single Mum, either.

When the court released my son it made Lily and me unbelievable happy. And even better, Alfie was released before I had to get mixed up with collecting money on the SPICE run. That would surely have got me into real trouble with the law.

A week or so after Dickie's funeral, a solicitor rang Alfie and asked him to call in to his office with his passport. I panicked as I was afraid there was a technical hitch with his release papers from the court, although he was sure it wasn't that. I had to keep myself busy when he went 'cos I wasn't up for any more bad news. I'd had my fair share of troubles and probably me mother's as well. I spent a couple of hours spring cleaning the house, but I couldn't put my mind to it.

And then Alfie came back from town grinning from ear to ear. He rushed through the door and picked me off me feet and swung me around like a windmill. I screamed with delight knowing that whatever it was, it wasn't bad news.

'Guess what?' he asked. Well I couldn't guess. How could I? Eventually I got the news out of him but not before he dashed to the corner shop and came back with four cans of

lager and a bottle of white wine for me. I knew this had to
be something special.

Alfie told me he could remember taking a large brown
envelope to the solicitors in town, not long before the fire
at Dickie's flat. He said he thought about steaming it open
at the time but couldn't be bothered. He was thinking it
might have been Dickie's will, but who cared because it
turned out he'd left everything to Alfie? My Alfie was so
excited that I joined in his happiness – it was impossible not
to. But actually, I never thought Dickie had much. He'd been
living off the social ever since he was beaten up on his way
home from the pub one night. It was such a brutal attack
that his legs never worked again and it seemed to age him
overnight; all the fight went out of him. I called on him now
and then, but Alfie told me I was a fool 'cos he'd ruined my
life. I thought that anything Dickie had to leave to Alfie
would have n burnt in his flat.

But it turned out I was wrong. Dickie had shares and gold
bars worth stashed away worth somewhere around three
hundred thousand pounds in all. Alleluia! That was
something to get yer head round, wasn't it? Lady Luck had
found out where we lived at last.

We were only allowed to see Alfie's daughter once a
month and I always tried to make it special. Livi loved my
Lily who was very sweet with her. We often went to the
park or down by the canal if the weather was OK and Lily
loved to push the pram. She'd change her nappies and feed
her and she'd even clear up her muddles. She was a right
little mother to her. Alfie took them both to the zoo a
couple of times and they went to the indoor pool too. I
always pushed the boat out for a nice tea and Alfie's little
girl seemed to fit in with us a treat.

One year Alfie asked if he could take Livi on holiday but
the snooty mother said no. She said they were off to the
'Isles of Scilly,' wherever they were so we didn't get much
of a look in during the school holidays. But we made the

best of it and I could see that having Olivia in his life could be the thing to make Alfie turn his life around.

There was a lot of money in Alfie's account after all the paperwork was done on Old Dickie's estate. Although my son claimed it was dirty money, I could see a way it would change our lives for ever. Alfie had taken himself off to college after his release from prison where he completed a motor mechanics course he'd started while he was inside. Alan helped him get a job when he finished and I was so proud of him. The job was poorly paid compared to dealing drugs, but Alfie swore all that was behind him now he had Livi to consider.

I did a bit of digging around on the net and found a perfect little car business for sale on the outskirts of Oxford. It wasn't far from where the posh ones had taken his daughter to live. There was a small flat above the garage workshop, big enough for Alfie and his daughter when she came to stay. Not that she'd been allowed to stay with us so far, but Alfie intended to go to court to get better access. If Alfie bought the business, I thought I'd swap my housing association flat for something nearer to him. I was buzzing with excitement which was rather an unusual feeling for me and I liked it.

Alan was still on the scene. We dated all through the first year Alfie came home. Lily loved him and we often went to his house for the weekend. But when he asked me to marry him I was scared shitless. I said no because I had no idea how to say yes. But we stayed friends and he is the nicest bloke I've ever known. I hope he asks me to marry him again 'cos I think I'd say yes if he did. I don't think he's bothered with other girls, so there's hope.

After a lot of nagging and getting my Lily on side, Alfie came with us to look at the garage. And he thought it looked OK. I thought it was brilliant, but tried to keep my excitement under wraps. I knew Alfie would take some persuading to make the move but I was thinking it would get him away from all his druggy mates and nearer to his daughter. Lily said she wouldn't mind moving school as long as it was soon 'cos she was getting close to secondary school. She also liked the idea of going to a new school where nobody knew her brother had been in prison. Of course, it would be good for me to leave a load of baggage behind, too. Moving away from Alan was the only thing that was not so good, but when I told him about it he said ten miles was nothing and we'd still keep seeing each other. He was excited for me and the kids and encouraged me to push Alfie into buying his own business.

You should have seen the estate agent's face when Alfie told her it was a cash sale. I felt like I was bloody Beyonce and I'd never been so happy in my life. It looked as though I was going to be a proper person at last, the sort of person who lived a decent life and could be a good mother. I'd hardly dared get used to being a grandma yet, in case the snooty ones on the estate took her away. Money always counts doesn't it, but we all enjoyed having little Livi when we could.

Lily loves her new school and I think she'll do well in her exams. She wants to be a nurse which makes me dead proud and I'll do anything to help her get there. We were so lucky to get a flat swap to Oxford and it's a better home than we left behind. I've found a job in a local factory making motorbike seats and I picked up the job real quick. The money is just enough to go round and I've got a little nest-egg which Alfie gave me from Dickie's money. I'm keeping it safe so that Lily can go to university.

'I'll pay my own way Mum.' Lily said when I told her. 'Just spend it on yourself.'

As if I'll do that.

I'm so proud of my Alfie; nobody would recognise him these days. He's even got a lad working for him on an apprentice scheme. He's got more work than he can handle and puts in long hours to get everything done.

We both worried about who would do his books when he bought the business, 'cos none of us had a clue about accounts. Luckily, the lady who'd done it before was happy to stay on, so Alfie just gets stuck into the cars that keep arriving for repair. He's talking about being an MOT centre in a couple of years.

I'm still waiting for something to spoil our new lives and have to pinch myself sometimes. Bit it's bound to have a hiccup, sooner or later 'cos we're not known for being lucky.

Mummy – you are going to find this hard and you'll think me a heartless bitch but...the thing is...I don't want Olivia. I don't want to be a mother...I want freedom to start a new life without her. I think it's time she was formally adopted, don't you?

Lottie

When our little family tipped up at the stately pile, I announced that we resembled fly-tippers. Tom was not even slightly amused. It took two large removal vans and two overloaded cars to get our possessions into their new home. Olivia was so excited she was sick when we sat down to lunch, so I put her down for her afternoon nap while I signposted the men to various rooms with our worldly goods.

Tom had made all the decisions about which rooms would become our private residence and what would be open to the public. My opinion was not required. But we needed more space than my mother-in-law, he announced, as she mostly confined herself to two rooms. I was happy with what I got. And as there was little spare cash, I set about revamping the ancient furnishings and with a little imagination, I achieved a comfortable home.

I've got used to overhearing visitor conversation in the rose garden and curious eyes gazing at our private apartment. But when I take Olivia for walks in the grounds we blend in so well that no one notices us. We encourage her to have friends over to play and often a noisy sleep-over has prompted my cautious husband to turn pale with fear for his ancestral antiques.

We are preparing for our fourth Christmas in Knoxbury Hall and Saskia is coming home. The roast is sizzling in the oven and lunch is well under way. I've chosen pork because it's Saskia's favourite and I know she rarely gets the chance to indulge. I remember my student days when pasta with sauce was pretty much my staple diet and nothing suggests that's changed.

'Granny, can I have some bird seed?'

'We fed them this morning,' I remind Olivia.

'Yes but the magpies ate most of it and the robin looks really hungry. He's on the wall and I think he's waiting to be fed.' Olivia's face falls and I can't resist her plea.

'OK, but you'll have to come and get it 'cos I'm busy cooking lunch for Mummy.'

'Only Mummy?' Can we all have some?'

I rustle her dark curls and notice the red highlights which are her only genetic nod to her mother. Without doubt she's Alfie's; he's passed on his soft brown skin and melting toffee eyes.

'Yes, we'll all have some,' I reply. 'Even Nathan likes roast pork.' I watch her eyes at the mention of Nate but she gives little away.

'Does Daddy like pork?'

'Probably. I think everyone likes it. Can you manage the lid on the birdseed?'

'I'm five in thirty more sleeps Granny. Have you forgotten?'

I bend to kiss my precious granddaughter and ask her not to be over-generous with the bird seed. She has a tendency to throw the lot at them when the weather is as cold as today and claims they're all starving. But what's a bit of bird seed in the greater scheme of things? Papa will help if you ask him,' I say.

'I can manage. I can do it.'

Of course she can. Ever since she crawled at eight months old she's been independent and now she's at school, she's romping away at an alarming rate.

I'm so looking forward to seeing Saskia. After she came through the coma unscathed I believed she was our own special. And although I'm not a believer in a greater being, I accept we were blessed with her recovery and try to remember it every day of my life. I'll never forget the very darkest days, the days when I was at breaking point; Tom and I were both imagining the worst but praying for the best and those prayers were answered. These days, it's hard to spoil her as we see her so seldom. When she chose to do her medical training in Exeter, it was inevitable she wouldn't get home too often, but she's coming home for Christmas. We're having two Christmas trees this year and they're in the stable block waiting for Saskia and Olivia to magic them into glowing, shimmering works of art.

I can hear the phone ringing and wipe my hands clean from peeling potatoes.

'Hi Mum. We're running about half an hour late. Sorry. Traffic's bad. We'll be another hour.'

'No probs Darling. I'll hold lunch. I haven't put the roasties in yet.'

'Mmm...I can smell them already. I'll get Nate to drive faster.'

'Safer. Tell him to drive safer. That's all that matters.'

'I know, I know. Just teasing. See you soon.'

I go outside to tell Olivia that her Mummy and Nate will be arriving in a while but she's totally engrossed in birdseed.

'Okay. Granny, do you think the magpies will eat all these seeds before the robin gets a chance? Shall I stand here and guard the bird table?'

I laugh. 'No Olivia, you can't do that. You'll frighten all the birds away if you stay outside.'

She frowns and is probably learning that life isn't always fair. 'Can Daddy come for lunch?'

'Not today. You're seeing Daddy on Boxing Day, remember?'

'Oh yes. And Lily. She told me she's going to have real makeup for Christmas. Do you believe her?'

'If she says so,' I say. 'She doesn't usually tell lies.'

'How does Father Christmas know about girl's makeup? He's a man.'

'Well, some men know a lot about makeup, or maybe some of the elves are girls. That would work.'

'Mmm. I never thought about that.'

We hurry indoors before the biting wind seeps up trouser legs and nibbles at delicate skin. I put on my festive CD and revel in the joy of the Eton Boys singing carols while peeling the potatoes. I remind Olivia the Snowman film is on the TV, but she declines in favour of her Lego.

I can hear Tom in the shower and he's cutting it a bit fine 'cos the kids will be here any minute. I've managed a quick stroke of lipstick and brushed my hair, but all the hallmarks of a busy cook are apparent on my face. I've held lunch back so that we can all have a drink when they arrive.

We don't know Nate very well, but we're pleased he's joining us for Christmas. But as Tom and I approve of him, it'll probably be a short-lived relationship. Saskia has had some gruesome fellas over the last few years and Alfie is included in the number. However, I take each day as it comes, as Mum would say. All Tom and I want for Saskia at the moment is to see her graduate and find a job that makes her happy.

I'm determined this Christmas will be perfect. I only have one shot at it as I think Saskia and Nathan are spending Boxing Day with his parents and the New Year in London with friends. London will undoubtedly be a more spirited venue than life in the Hanson household. Mum and Dad will make it for Christmas lunch but they'll need to get back for the milking. They are starting to show their age and I've dared to suggest they might consider retirement. Dad will need some persuading to give up the farm which represents his lifetimes' work although I think Mum can see the advantages of not having their lives ruled by the needs of the livestock. Tom suggested they may like to settle on the estate, but that is all for discussion after Christmas.

I can hear a car and call Olivia away from her Lego creation.

'Do you think Mummy will like it? A frown of concentration ruckles her face.

'I'm sure she will. Quick. They're here.'

There's a bundle of cuddles and hellos in the hallway and everyone is shining with the glow of Christmas. Saskia lifts her daughter sky-high and makes her scream with laughter.

'I'm nearly five Mummy. I'm not a baby.' When she arrives at floor level she wraps her arms around her mother's hips and hugs her. 'I've missed you Mummy. You haven't even seen my Lego'.

'In a while. Let me get inside Baby.'

'It's huge and I did it all myself. She catches Tom's eye, 'well most of it. Papa helped a bit, didn't you Papa?

'I did, but most of the work was done by you.' Tom is generous to a fault where his granddaughter is concerned.

I edge everyone into the sitting room before they can congregate in the kitchen and Tom is already taking orders for drinks. Nate has gone to bring in their luggage from the car and I give Saskia another hug. It's great to have her home, even if I have to share her these days.

'Look Mummy. Look. Do you like it?'

'Saskia bends to take the Lego from her daughter's hand. 'I love it Poppet. You are a clever girl. Maybe you'll be a doctor like Mummy, when you're older.'

'Do you make people better?'

'Not yet, but in a couple of years' time I shall. Nate will be making people better next year. How cool is that?'

Olivia is unimpressed and I'm slightly edgy. I know my daughter well and I'm picking up a vibe I can't analyse.

She's slightly spikey and I'm wondering why. But I leave them to it and return to the kitchen to make the gravy.

'Do you want your usual, Darling?' Tom calls.

'Please. Not too strong.'

Saskia joins me. 'Olivia is really into her Lego isn't she? Clever little sausage.'

'She loves building things.' A wash of sadness reminds me how little Saskia knows about her daughter. Sometimes it's as if she's her tiresome kid sister who has a tendency to get in her way.

Tom brings me a gin and tonic flushed with ice. 'I've left yours in the sitting room Saskia. Shall I bring it?'

'I expect Olivia wants to show-off her princess drawings,' I interrupt. 'She's got a whole drawer of them waiting to show Mummy.' I know I sound pushy. I want Saskia to want to spend time with her daughter, but see little sign of it.

'No thanks Dad. I'll go and find Nate.'

I avoid Tom's eyes and concentrate on getting food to the table while it's piping hot.

Lunch is a success. The roast is much admired and large appetites sated. Except Olivia, who allows her mother to cut up her pork, appeases her by spooning broccoli onto her plate, but eats little. She pushes her lunch around the plate until it resembles soup and rarely takes her eyes off Nate. It's hardly surprising she feels jealous of her mother's latest boyfriend.

Saskia and Nate want to pop into town after lunch to finish their Christmas shopping. Olivia is not invited.

'I have no idea what to buy the man who has everything. Any ideas for Dad,' Saskia asks while I scrape plates.

We have this conversation every year and each Christmas it gets harder. The truth is, he'd be happy with a box of Scilly Fudge from Michelle on St Mary's, but that feels inadequate for a father for Christmas. 'Why don't you get him a jumper from M&S?' I hear myself suggesting the default item which can never be called exciting, by any stretch of the imagination. 'You could send for some fudge.'

'I'm sure I'll find something.' She swings her pine-green, hand-knitted scarf around her auburn hair and kisses my cheek. A whirl of winter leaves rush the hallway as they go.

'I didn't want to go. If Mummy had asked me, I didn't want to go.'

I feel a squeeze on my heartstrings. 'I need you here Darling. We have to wrap Mummy's present and you can do your best writing on her card. She'll be so surprised how well you can write, won't she?'

'Have we got a present for Nate?'

'We have. Just something small. Would you like to see what it is?'

We climb the stairs to the spare room which has a duffel bag and two carrier bags of stuff dumped on the floor. I peek inside Saskia's room and it looks like a Medina. They're sleeping together, of course. After all the shenanigans when Saskia was sixteen, it seems useless to be prissy about their sleeping arrangements now.

'Is Daddy's present in here? I need to wrap it and write a card for him, too. Did we buy Lily anything?'

I sigh. It doesn't get any easier. Well, maybe just a little. At least I can look Alfie Collins in the eye and know he didn't bestow permanent damage on our daughter. But I need more than that, these days. I want my granddaughter to have a more settled life. I don't want her to be the odd one out, the one without her Mother around, the one who drifts between us and her father. Tom tells me 'blended families' are the norm these days, but I see Olivia as part of a fragmented family. And I wanted so much more for her. It seems the longer she and her mother live apart, the cooler their relationship becomes. No surprises there.

When Olivia was born I could see the spark between Saskia and Alfie was already extinguished. Saskia was tired of him, as I predicted, although I knew Alfie felt differently about her. So why, I asked myself, did he have to have access to our granddaughter. I felt it would have been different if they were together; then I'd have had to get use to the yob visiting our home. But Saskia was belligerent and it was not up for discussion.

I had no conscience about fighting with every dirty trick I knew to persuade our daughter to change her mind. I felt a clean break was the easier option, certainly for Tom and me who would be bringing Olivia up for the foreseeable future. But Saskia would not be moved. Alfie Collins would have access to his daughter and I had to make some kind of deal with my anger. I'd got my daughter back so it had to be give and take, I reasoned. I'd made deals with God after all, so this was probably pay-back time. Tom took the moral high ground with an unspoken *'told you so.'*

But the aggravation didn't stop with Alfie Collins because Tracey claimed her rights as a grandmother, too. And it was at this point, I realised Churchill's College had turned me into a snob. For whatever reason, I didn't want my precious grandchild to be tarnished by the likes of that family. Apparently Olivia was shown to them as a small baby on one of Alfie's access visits and there'd been regular contact since. I'm told they were both welcomed into Tracey's home, 'like part of the family.' Saskia told me, 'the house is spotless Mum. And they really love Olivia.' Hmm... I hated the world at that moment and made no more deals with God.

Saskia and Nate have returned with arms full of presents and Olivia's excitement is palpable.

'Are they for me Mummy? Are they all for me?'

'No you little minx. Father Christmas brings your presents, doesn't he?'

'Only some. You have to buy me some too. Have you forgotten?' Her little face crumpled.

Suddenly the flood-gates opened and she sobbed into my skirt. 'Granny said some presents come from Father Christmas and some from Mummy and Daddy.' I received a dark look from under her eyelashes which called me a liar. 'Do you think Daddy has forgotten me, too?'

I meet Saskia's eyes and see her fear. She has no idea how to handle her daughter.

'Darling, in some families it's Granny and Papa who buy presents. That's what happens when Mummies are busy.'

'Are you sure?' Her little chin is still wobbling.

'Quite sure and I don't want any peeping when I wrap them up. Do you promise?'

She gives me a hug. 'You're the best Granny. And Papa.' She turns to Tom, 'Did you buy me a present too?'

'I did Angel. You can be sure your pile of presents will be mountain-high.' He raises his arms to the heavens and placates our grandchild. Olivia brightens immediately. She smiles and hugs Tom as if her life depended upon him. 'Thank you Papa. Thank you.'

Saskia helps me wrap Olivia's presents on Christmas Eve. It's lovely to have my daughter to myself and I ask her about uni. It's a safe subject. I try not to be too inquisitive about her life, but after nursing her back to health, I find it impossible to forget her lack of judgement on that fateful night. Tom and I think Nate is a steadying influence and hope the relationship survives Christmas and New Year. Don't they say stress levels at this time of year can impact on relationships? I think Nate will be doing something without Saskia after New Year so, hopefully, we shall have our daughter all to ourselves for a few days, which is just as well as I know something is brewing. I can't pinpoint the issue and I don't think it's between Saskia and Nate, so it's either her training or her daughter. I just pray she isn't pregnant.

Tracey

My Alfie still loves that girl. I've told him to get out and find a new one but he says all his effort's going into his business and his daughter. He's doing dead good at both. He's built the business up and I'm real proud of him.

Rita Trotman

It's been a bit of a long haul these last few years. I don't
think I'll ever get over the stress of those months after Alfie
was arrested. They've left permanent scars on me. And
then there was Dickie's death. Silly old sod left a ciggy
burning and it caught the chair alight. They didn't get him
out in time and as his legs were already knackered, he must
have burned to a crisp. My Alfie said it was no more than he
deserved, but I wouldn't go that far. Funny thing was, it
turned out Dickie had all that money and gold hidden away.
Who'd have thought that?

Ever since he got out, Alfie's stayed clean 'cos his daughter
means everything to him. Looks like he's turned his life
around. In fact, we all have. And Old Dickie's money was a
Godsend, even though Alfie called it dirty money. But I kept
nagging. I told him it was the only chance he was likely to
get to make something of his life and who cared what
colour the money was? For once he listened to me.

Livi is coming to our house on Boxing Day. Well, actually
it's to Alfie's flat but Lily and me will be there when she
arrives. I can't wait. We'll have another Christmas Day just
for my granddaughter and Lily has hidden little gifts for her
in the Christmas tree. Hope the whole bleeding lot don't
come down while she's looking!

Lottie

Our fourth Christmas at Knoxbury Hall was a joy and while
Olivia slowly warmed to Nate, her relationship with Saskia
dropped into a familiar rhythm. We trod the usual road of
over-indulgence, silly hats and inane television and by
Christmas night we were all exhausted. I confessed to being
relieved that Saskia and Nate were going to his parents the
following day, but I stressed about Olivia spending Boxing
Day with Alfie. Something still curdled in my stomach at the
mention of his name. When Saskia put Olivia to bed I heard
her say she and Nate were leaving in the morning and they

176

would take her to Daddy's around ten o'clock. That meant either Alfie would return her to us, or we'd have to fetch her. Neither was an easy option.

Boxing Day breakfast was a quiet affair consisting predominately of coffee. Olivia suggested we share the left-over trifle but was soon dissuaded when she found an unopened present in the dining room. It was lovely to have my family around me and I felt showered in riches because they were all safe and happy. It hadn't always been so.

'See you in a few days.' Saskia, Nate and Olivia waved from the car and with a crunch of gravel they were gone.

'I really must get John to sweep these paths.'

My husband noticed imperfections that I thought were normal life. Tom was never off duty now we the estate to care for. I was thinking the bloody leaves could wait, and anyway, who could expect staff to work on Boxing Day? For me the dampener was Alfie Collins who would return our granddaughter in a few hours.

As usual after a family Christmas, the analysis followed.

'Great food Snooks. You really pushed the boat out and you deserve a few days of peace and quiet.'

'Wasn't it lovely to have her home? Don't you think she seems more grounded since she's been with Nate?'

'If I was a betting man I'd say he's the one. Their relationship feels close to me. But I'm only a man, so I could be wrong!'

'Well I hope you're right, on this occasion.'

'They could have a great life together.'

'Did you get the feeling Saskia wants to talk to us about something? Did you pick up a slightly....I don't know, but I think something is afoot.'

'Can't say I did. She seemed perfectly normal to me.'

I can sense the game is changing and my heart tells me we'll soon be major players in our granddaughter's life. I can't see how Olivia is ever going to fit with her mother's ambitions. Nate was sweet with her but it's a big ask of any fellow to take on another man's child. And I can't help thinking about the long hours both of them will have to work in hospital.

Tom loves his granddaughter in a way that is heaven to watch. He taught her to read and can't resist getting in the pool and encouraging her to shed the water wings. She's brought out a softer side to him. If I ponder the abortion issue, which I sometimes do, I remember the tenacity with which I nurtured that baby in Saskia's womb. I'm sure Tom is pleased it was an argument he lost.

On Boxing Day evening it was me who opened the door to Alfie Collins and Olivia and I could see she was hyped on sugar.

'Granny, I want to show Daddy my presents from Father Christmas.'

What could I do? I opened the door wide enough for him to come in and left Olivia to show him to her room.

'Well done Snooks. He doesn't bite does he?' Tom handed me a large gin and tonic.

'He didn't, but he looks as if he might.'

'Come on love. It's been nearly five years and he is her father.'

'I know and I feel guilty. Maybe we should offer him a drink. It is Christmas.'

'Hell must have frozen over Lottie! OK. I'll catch him as he comes downstairs with Olivia. It'll please her, for sure.'

It was probably the hardest half hour since Saskia's coma. Alfie accepted our invitation to have a beer and followed Tom into the drawing room. I think a nod was forthcoming from me, but I can't be sure.

'I've had a great day with Livi. She played with my kid sister and we took her to feed the ducks. I wrapped her up warm.' He looked at me. 'Mum loves to see her.'

There was one of those awkward silences I'd learned to deal with all those years ago. I just looked back at Alfie Collins who, if anything, was even better looking than when I saw him in court. Except for his grimy fingernails; probably they were achieved curtesy of his mechanic's job. I'd heard on the grape vine he was doing well with his business and who could begrudge him that?

'She's got a load of presents in the car. Shall I get them?'

He looked as if a quick escape would be a blessing. But I heard myself say, 'why don't you finish you beer first? Did you have a good Christmas?'

He pinned me with those chocolate eyes and for the first time I could see how he attracted Saskia. His daughter stayed close to his side and he ruffled her hair and stroked her cheek as he talked.

'Yeh, it was great. Mum's not much of a cook but we had a turkey ready by five o'clock. I gave her a microwave for Christmas but she hasn't worked out how to use it yet.'

'Business good is it? Tom sounded as if he was really interested, an attribute which comes as standard if Churchill's is in your bloodline.

'Doing great, thanks. Month by month the turnover's rising..... I'm doing a simple book keeping course at Tech.'

'Ah, commendable.'

With that Alfie gulped his beer and placed the glass on a table. 'Thanks for that.' He picked up his daughter and kissed her. I've got to go now Rascal. But I'll see you soon. OK?'

Olivia started to cry.

'Don't cry Poppet. Come with Daddy to get your presents out of the car. You can show Granny and Grandpa.'

'You mean Papa. He's called Papa.'

'Exacting little miss, aint you?'

I could feel the chill in the hall as he left the door ajar. He gave Olivia a shopping bag from Aldi which was full of her gifts and I heard him tell her to hurry indoors before she got cold.

And then he was gone. I looked at Tom for reaction, but he was inscrutable.

During the midweek lull between Christmas and New Year, that annual slump when everyone has over-indulged, I can think of nothing but adopting Olivia. It makes perfect sense

179

and I know Tom will be OK with it, too. But he keeps telling me not to jump the gun as Saskia has yet to put the idea to us. But I know she will and I can barely contain my excitement. I have a million plans in my head, just waiting to be put into practice when I'm a Mum again. What a precious gift she'll be.

Saskia is coming home after New Year for a few days before she returns to uni so it will be the perfect time to set things in motion. I can see several positives around the logistics, not least, that Olivia won't need to change her surname. Hanson is on her birth certificate and she'll be a Hanson until she marries. But the most important point is not the legal process or how Tom and I feel, it has to be about Olivia and how she might adapt to the new arrangements. Will Olivia feel rejected by her mother? Only time will tell. And I can't think about Alfie Collins having access to his daughter as that will mar my excitement and God knows, I deserve a little bit of good luck to go my way.

Over the last five years I've carved a niche for myself on the estate, despite having little input into Tom's initial ideas. He spent more time than I thought healthy consulting his mother when we first moved. And he continues to visit her each day for his afternoon tea. I don't receive an invite thank God, and Olivia avoids her like the plague.

But the time Tom spent with his mother paid dividends because she grudgingly agreed to the proposed changes. There was a proviso, however, that the public were not to stray within twenty metres of her house. I could understand her concerns about the public tramping all over her senior years, but Tom ensured she was happy when we drew his ideas on large sheets of paper. We wanted to put a one way system in place so that visitors would enter and exit through the main gates where a huge car parking area was created from one of the meadows. The planners were amazingly receptive to our ideas, so there were few delays with starting the new business.

The Grand Dame made one effort to welcome us to the Hall which morphed into the teatime from hell. Olivia was ten months old and wound up with excitement; she refused to sit still, no matter how much I coaxed. The little monkey threw the proffered biscuit onto the floor which Tom dutifully scrabbled to retrieve from under an antique table. I nibbled a cucumber sandwich with my granddaughter firmly wedged on one knee.

Before the occasion could deteriorate further, I drank half a cup of Earl Grey which I detest, thanked the host for her hospitality and muttered apologies before taking Olivia home. Black marks for both of us that day and we've never been invited to the lodge since. I have, on several occasions, invited my mother-in-law to Sunday lunch at the Hall, but she churlishly declines to join us for Christmas. Too many memories lie within, apparently, and I quietly celebrate my good fortune.

I oversee the daily stream of visitors and the bevy of attractions we've created to part them from their money. We're blessed with good staff for the café which serves homemade delights created on site by the indomitable Eileen. I need to be strong around her feather-light Victoria sandwiches and the homemade fudge is a forbidden fruit.

A local lady called Grace was found to help with Olivia, and not only is she flexible about her hours, but she is much admired by our granddaughter. Even though Olivia is now at school, we're able to employ Grace elsewhere on the estate until the school holidays come around. All appears to be back on an even keel for the family and I'm more than grateful for that.

Mummy... this is going to be tough but...Alfie wants to have care and custody of Olivia and...I've told him he can have her. The thing is, he's her father and although you've been wonderful, I think it best if she goes to Alfie. He's her blood relation and....I know how it feels to have no blood relations. Sorry if I'm causing you and Daddy pain. I thought maybe you would like to keep Olivia until after her birthday while Alfie deals with the custody papers. If it makes it easier, I'll come up from Exeter to take her to Alfie, when the time comes.

Tracey

I can hardly believe our good news. We've never had much good luck in our family but it's dropped like manna from heaven today. That snooty girl (I suppose now I shall have to pretend I like her 'cos of what she's done,) is letting my Alfie have custody of his daughter. I can't get my head around it but he's already said Lily and me can have his flat and he's looking for a house with a mortgage for the two of them to live in. I told him it needs to be close to the business so that I can help with Livi. It's been a real pinch-me couple of days.

I shan't give notice on the flat we're in at the moment 'cos I think it will take a while to sort the legal stuff. But I can't believe Lily and me will be living in my Alfie's property. It's the first time we haven't been in social housing for the whole of our lives and it's gonna be great.

I don't want Lily to have to change school again 'cos she's doing so well. She needs to stay where she is until she's done her GCSE's. If she wants to be a nurse she'll need to stay on for A levels but all that is something for the future. I can't get used to the warm feeling I've got in my stomach. I worry that somebody will take it away from me.

Alan and me are still an item. And he's still nice to me which is the best thing about it. I thought when we first started going out that he'd turn into a rat, like most men I've ever known. But he's different. I wish I was brave enough to tell him I'd like to marry him now.

Lottie

My daughter is a Judas...well that's how it feels. I'm more furious than I've ever been in my life. Anger is sitting like a metal coil in my chest and those night time elves have come back to torment. I know part of my mental state is shock as I was convinced Olivia would soon be ours. But mostly, I'm bloody furious with my daughter. How can she drop this on us after all we've done for her? Olivia feels like our own and that's partly due to the lack of interest her mother has shown in her wellbeing.

Saskia gave me a load of crap when I challenged her decision to give her daughter away. She denied she was 'giving her away' and tried to tell me Olivia needed to live with the only blood relative who wanted her. Apparently, it's Saskia's intention to permanently bow out of her daughter's life to pursue the life she wants, which doesn't include a child. But how can it be better for Olivia to live with a man who is at best, a ruffian?

I'm not good when life gets beyond my control as I'm a Capricorn and I need to know what's happening and why. Sadly, I'm unable to submerge hostile thoughts about my daughter who has never regained her closeness to me since the coma. But how could she do this to us? Tom and I are determined she won't get away with it, although we're not fighting for ourselves, but to protect Olivia's best interests. How can it be better for her to be dragged from the only home she's known to stay with a family living on the breadline?

It looks as if we are going to meet bloody Alfie Collins in court again. Our solicitor thinks we have a good case and that Olivia's best interest is served by her staying with us. But it's what the judge decides that really matters. I'm strong as a bulldog about this and there will be none of the wishy-washy Lottie, as seen when Saskia was ill. I know we're going to win.

Because I am so angry with my daughter we are out of contact at the moment although I noticed her allowance is

still dropping into her bank account. It's usual for her to
come home at Easter but I can't find it in my heart to invite
her and Nate to stay this year. It feels hypocritical and sad
in equal measure. And does Olivia need to gobble her
Easter bunnies with a mother who is about to abandon her?
I don't think so.

Heidi Brooker rang me yesterday and as usual, she can
always lighten anyone's mood. She told me all the gossip
from Churchill's including details of the new Head of Art
who has a pierced nose and a boy who has announced he's
gender neutral. OMG. Neither of us can believe either will
be accepted by the establishment and we certainly had a
giggle.

Heidi talks a lot of sense and she came up with a good idea
to help us gain custody of Olivia. I'm not sure Tom is keen,
but he agreed anything is worth a try. As I know too well,
his quiet manner hides deep waters and I think he fears
Alfie may win custody of his daughter if it goes to court,
especially now he's turned his life around. The family
appear to have come into some money and they look on
the respectable side of rough, which Tom feels may bias the
court case in their favour.

So my friend Heidi Brooker is the reason I'm outside a
block of housing association flats on the outskirts of Oxford;
I have a dry mouth but spade loads of confidence. I also
have a list of incentives which I'll offer one by one, until I
make a breakthrough with our plans. This has to work.

The grubby door is opened by the same mousey woman
who sat on the end of the row at the court case. The one I
noticed crying. She's petite and looks good enough without
makeup. I see from her face that she knows who I am.

"Spose you'd better come in.'

I thank her and enter a neat, almost tasteful sitting room
with photos of Olivia and an older girl displayed in various
vantage points. That feels bloody strange and for one
minute I slide of piste. But I gather myself together and sit

where indicated by the almost shy lady who is clearly surprised to find me on her doorstep.

'I've come about Olivia, which I'm sure you've guessed.'

I get no reaction but give the silence a chance to develop into something verbal. It doesn't, so I take the initiative. 'It's about the custody….the court case….My husband and I wondered…'

''Spose *you* want to keep her.'

I didn't expect such bluntness but I agreed that was why I'd come.

'My Alfie is dead set on getting her. He's her Dad, so she should be with him. Seeing as her mother don't want her.'

'Ouch! But I remember my arguments. 'We are her stability…we're all she's known. I've brought her up from the hour she was born. I even….fought to ensure she wasn't aborted. I think I have…a good case to keep her too.'

Tracey slid her hair behind her ears and I thought how young she looked. I nodded to the photos….'Is that your daughter with Olivia?'

'Yeh. Dead proud of my Lily, I am.'

'How old is she?'

'Fourteen, going on twenty four!'

'I know what a handful teenage girls can be. Saskia was never easy and when…the problem…the drugs and the coma hit our family, I was devastated that I hadn't been able to keep her safe. That's what mothers want, isn't it? To keep their children safe?'

Tracey looked at me and I could see she was softening. I could see a glimmer of sympathy. 'The thing is Tracey, I wondered if you could persuade Alfie to come to an agreement whereby we kept Olivia but he had generous access. That way she'd have all of us in her life.'

'My Alfie thinks he'll win her in court.'

'But it isn't about winning is it? It's about what's best for Olivia.'

Tracey appeared to digest my thoughts for a few minutes while I soaked up the silence.

'But I was going to help with her. You know, pick her up from school and things.'

'I think Olivia would hate to change schools. She's really settled and…

'Think our schools aren't good enough?'

'Tracey, this isn't a contest. This is real life for Olivia and all of us wanting the best for her. How can taking her from us at the age of five and plonking her into a different family be good for her?'

'You mean she's better off in a posh family than living with the likes of us?'

'I didn't come here to fight. I came here to avoid a fight in court. It's bound to get brutal and haven't we all been hurt enough?'

'How much access was you thinking?'

'How much do you think would be fair?'

She thought for a minute or two. 'Every other weekend and taking her on holiday each year. Not sure what Alfie would say but…'

'Why don't you try it? We'd pay for everything she needs. Her clothes and any school bits and pieces.'

For some reason Tracey looked at her watch and the talking was over.

'I'll think about it. Give me yer phone number and I'll think about it.'

'Thank you. I can't ask for more than that.' I wrote my mobile number on a piece of paper she gave me and before I could say another word I was out of the door and wondering what I'd said to be ousted so abruptly.

And then I knew. Alfie was locking his car as I got into mine and I realised it had been a close run thing if she didn't want Alfie to see me.

It wasn't easy to keep our granddaughter. It felt like the second time I'd fought for her life and this time I was wading through treacle. Tracey and I met several times and at each meeting, I thought the atmosphere warmed a little. I got her around to agreeing what was best for Olivia, although relaxation of access was essential if we had any hope of keeping her. I reasoned that having some of my little girl was better than losing her to Alfie. Of course, I'd given no thought to Saskia's views on this, but I wanted an agreement from the Collins family before I approached my daughter.

I reasoned that if Alfie's bid to have Olivia was dropped, then Saskia would obviously want to leave her with Tom and me. Once more I was walking on eggshells but I'd do anything to keep that little girl. After negotiating further, Tracey went to work on her son. Inevitably, I had to meet with him and he was reluctant to agree with our plans, but made the point that when she was older she could choose where she lived. I agreed, having no doubt about where that would be.

The outcome of my request to the Collins family inevitably caused heartache. I'd seen it coming but had no ammunition to ward it off. Alfie bargained hard when it went down to the wire and I capitulated to the point where he has Olivia for half of all school holidays as well as every other weekend. I did make a proviso that if Olivia, for any reason, did not want to visit her father, then I would not force her. I hoped I'd covered all bases. Tracey did a great job and I'll forever be grateful to her for persuading her son to find a middle way that was best for his daughter. I was allergic to any more fighting and happy to have found a compromise.

I asked Alfie to let Saskia know about his decision. I knew it was cowardly but they were making life-changing decisions about their child so it seemed right. Quite how he gave her the information I have no idea but Saskia sent a putrid email to me saying she wanted nothing more to do with us. Her parting shot was that we couldn't adopt Olivia, although she could stay with us for the 'foreseeable future.'

I pine for the loss of my daughter and hope my granddaughter will never make me regret the sacrifice. Tom promises me Saskia will calm down, and maybe she will, but the chasm inside me is deep. Why does life have to be so bloody complicated?

And so a five year old little girl is taking the changes to her life with little resistance. Olivia finds Lily a big attraction when she visits her father and they go the extra mile to do things that please her. I wonder how long that can last and hope they fall into a more manageable routine. Next Christmas it's already agreed that Olivia will be with the Collins family and if we have no breakthrough with Saskia, then we will be a lonely twosome for the festive season. In my quiet moments, I convince myself that life is so much richer with Olivia in it than if she'd been aborted. I firmly believe I made the right decision although Tom would not agree since the fall out with our daughter. He thinks one child has been sacrificed for the other. Brutal.

I involve myself in the business which is busier than ever and try not to think of the problems too much. Tom argues that we had the best deal possible, in view of Saskia's insistence that Alfie remained in Olivia's life. He even told me I'd done an excellent job of keeping Olivia with us; he knows he could never have negotiated with the Alfie.

So here we are. Our daughter, who is not speaking to us, still manages to convey her need for money. Email is a wonderful, faceless form of communication. Saskia always contacts Tom for her needs as I suspect she finds it impossible to deal with my misery and anger. She knows me well and I can't help thinking of the early years when our heartbeats were one and the same. She probably copes by keeping me out of mind. I'm going to leave it another couple of months and then I shall contact Nate. Maybe he can provide a sliver of hope for reconciliation.

Every Easter and summer Saskia has worked on the estate to earn money for her life in Exeter. We, of course pay all her tuition fees but the additional needs surrounding a medical degree are substantial. She's made no attempt to come home and Easter has already come and gone.

It was a June day, just a few weeks ago, when my mobile interrupted restocking the cake stand for Eileen. My stomach did a flip as I recognised Saskia's number and I downed everything to take her call.

'Mum......Mummy I.....'

'What is it Darling. I can't hear you through the tears. Come on, it can't be so bad. We can sort anything together.'

'Yes, but I've been such a cow to you and Daddy....I.....'

'Yes but you're our own special cow, aren't you?' I heard a stifled laugh through the tears.

'Can we come home next weekend? Me and Nate?' I stifled a desire to correct her grammar. 'You never need to ask Honey. Of course you can.'

'I'm so sorry Mummy. Really sorry.....Do you forgive me?'

'Shh....come home and we'll sort it all out. Olivia will be thrilled to see you.'

'OK. Would you do roast pork on Sunday?'

'Of course Darling. Just drive carefully. Big hugs to you both.'

I'm fixating on the pork. Not dreaming of what she might say or any news she may have. I'm concentrating only on what I know, which is our daughter is coming home where she belongs.

Rita Trotman

28954528R00112

Printed in Poland
by Amazon Fulfillment
Poland Sp. z o.o., Wrocław